SECOND HONEYMOON

The holidays are looming for Jenni
Fielding, and her son and daughter
have their own ideas about where
they want to spend them. So too
does Jenni's husband, Chris, whose
ideas for their second honeymoon
come as rather a shock to his
devoted wife. All ends well — but
not quite as the family expected!

Books by Vivien Young
in the Linford Romance Library:

JENNI

VIVIEN YOUNG

SECOND HONEYMOON

Complete and Unabridged

LINFORD
Leicester

First Linford Edition
published December 1992

British Library CIP Data

Young, Vivien
Second honeymoon.—Large print ed.—
Linford romance library
I. Title II. Series
823.914 [F]

ISBN 0-7089-7296-9

Published by
F. A. Thorpe (Publishing) Ltd.
Anstey, Leicestershire
Set by Words & Graphics Ltd.
Anstey, Leicestershire
Printed and bound in Great Britain by
T. J. Press (Padstow) Ltd., Padstow, Cornwall

With much love to my daughter Judi, wishing her a happy 'second honeymoon'.

1

MOST stories come to an end with wedding bells. Well, this story begins with them. It was the wedding of my friend Jill to her fiance Robert Durham, on a beautiful day in April, in a dear little country church. My daughter Cathy was to be her bridesmaid, and my husband Chris, my son Tony and myself had all been invited to the wedding.

Cathy had been going round for days warbling "Here comes the bri-ide" and stealing surreptitious peeps at the dress she was to wear, a most unusual and original conception in white, trimmed with black, delightfully feminine with flounces and frills. Even though Cathy's usual outfit for her leisure time consisted of jeans and sweatshirt, she wasn't able to resist the lure of looking ravishingly pretty for Jill's wedding, and I considered that Jill had probably changed the course of world history by persuading my thirteen-year-old pop fan daughter to appear publicly in a skirt.

Jill herself was to wear a glorious cream voile affair, with a picture hat trimmed with one red rose and long red ribbons. I, somewhat more humbly, had a simple but attractive pale blue suit with a beret that perched on one side of my head á la Veronica Lake.

"Who's Veronica Lake?" Cathy asked blankly, when she saw it.

"She was a bit before your time," I began, and Chris intervened:

"A bit before *your* time too, wasn't she, darling?"

"Well, fashions sort of go round in circles," I explained defensively. "That kind of look is back in now."

"Good grief! I suppose you don't want me to appear in a white raincoat and do a Humphrey Bogart?" enquired Chris, with interest.

I grinned. "I don't think that will be

necessary. Jill won't want her wedding photos to look like a scene from an old movie. Your grey suit will be fine."

So we were all set for the Great Day, and I woke to see that it was going to be a perfect morning. Dew lay on the grass of the lawn, and the garden was vivid with spring flowers. Chris was still sleeping peacefully, but I felt too excited to go back to bed, even though it was quite early, so I went stealthily downstairs to make myself a cup of coffee, and sat drinking it in my dressing-gown while I thought about all the events that had led up to this thrilling morning.

Until a few months before, I had led a harmless and peaceful existence, thoroughly enjoying my role as house-wife and mother. Then had come the advent of Henrietta, our new next-door-neighbour, who had bull-dozed me into appearing with the local Amateur Operatic Society by means of subtle flattery and tank-like persistence. I had actually stood up on the stage of the George B. Macdonald Hall in town and played the part of Maria in *The Sound of Music*, to admiring audiences. Admittedly, I had declared afterwards that nothing would ever induce me to appear on the stage again, but I had quite enjoyed it at the time, and it was through the Society that I had met Jill, who had played the role of Elsa. Even more important, it was through *The Sound of Music* that Jill had met Robert, and now we were actually going to their wedding!

I went into the living-room and absently removed the cover from the cage where the two feathered inhabitants of our house, Sophocles and Electra, spent their busy little days.

"Hello, Sophocles," I greeted them cheerfully. "Hello, Electra. Lovely morning for a wedding, isn't it?"

Electra immediately assumed her favourite position hanging upside-down from the top bars, but Sophocles, who was bright blue, fixed me with a piercing black eye and squawked back:

4

"Dead brill!"

That was his new trick, which he had learned from Cathy. Previously, he had only been able to say "Bee-uti-ful", but he had amazed us all by picking up Cathy's current expressions of delight, and now repeated them when ever he could.

"It's a good job Naomi didn't come back from America and hear him," Cathy said, the first time Sophocles astounded us with his cleverness. The budgies had belonged to her school friend Naomi Jones-Evans, who had gone to America to accompany her professor father on a lecture tour, and she had asked us to look after them while she was away. Later, she wrote that they had decided to stay and live in the States, so we had unanimously voted to keep the little birds. By then, they had become part of the family, and now it seemed as if they had been with us for ever.

But Naomi was a very serious-minded girl, and, as Cathy had pointed out, it was doubtful whether she would have approved of Sophocles talking slang.

"I don't think she'd have minded if he'd learned to say 'Eureaka', or — well, something like that," I agreed, and Tony grinned.

"Probably her idea was to eventually teach him to recite Pythagoras's Theorem."

But Sophocles had regrettably low standards.

"I don't think he'll even get an 'O' Level," said Chris, mock-seriously.

"But we love them as they are, don't we, then?" crooned Cathy into the cage, and they preened their feathers at her attention.

"Little pets!" I said fondly. You can see that we are rather silly about our two feathered friends.

However, I didn't have all the morning to spend talking to Sophocles and Electra.

"You'll have to excuse me today," I told them, as I made my way to the kitchen. "But I have a wedding to go to."

Eventually, we were all ready, standing round in our finery while Chris got out the car. Tony was the last to enter the living-room, looking most unlike himself in — actually — a suit, a shirt and tie, with his blond hair neatly brushed.

I blinked at him, my heart swelling with pride.

"To think," I murmured reminiscently, "that once you were a chubby little lad splashing about in your bath with your toy boats. I can't believe it." I shook my head dazedly.

"I mean, look at you now."

"Not too bad, am I?" he suggested smugly. In fact, he was a devastating eighteen. He put an arm round my shoulders.

"But I must admit, you look quite ravishing yourself, Mum."

"D'you think so?" I asked, flattered.

"Not a day over fifty!" Tony said airily, and I gave him a thump.

"Oh, Tony! You know I'm only thirty-seven!" I said indignantly. Then I looked round at them again and my heart melted. "Still, I love you both very much."

Cathy looked exasperatedly at the ceiling at such a display of maternal emotion, but Tony said tolerantly:

"Ah, well. I expect it's because we're all going to a wedding. You've got such a romantic nature, Mum. I expect you'll cry all through the ceremony."

But in fact, I didn't. I managed to keep the lump in my throat firmly under control as Jill floated up the aisle looking like a vision in cream, with Cathy following decorously behind her. As she passed, Cathy winked at me, and I couldn't help grinning to myself.

At first, Cathy had been overwhelmed to be asked to be Jill's bridesmaid, but now that the great moment had come, she was cheerfully blasé about the whole thing. However, she performed her part admirably, and when we saw

Jill's wedding photos later, everybody commented on how angelic my darling daughter looked, standing demurely at Jill's side with a posy of white flowers in her hands.

★ ★ ★

The reception went off beautifully, and I swam in a daze of champagne through the speeches, and dabbed at my eyes as Jill and Robert exchanged a kiss when they joined hands to cut the wedding cake. How beautifully romantic it all was! My own wedding day seemed so very far away, but when we got home and lounged about in a sort of anti-climax, I searched through the sideboard for my own Wedding Album, and turned the pages mistily.

"The Greatest Day of my Life! Remember it, Chris?"

"I remember your youngest bridesmaid getting locked in the loo," said Chris, reminiscently, and grinned. "We had to break the door down to rescue her."

"I wish I'd been there," giggled Cathy, who was now herself again in jeans and sweatshirt.

"Darling, you weren't born until several years later," I pointed out logically, turning another page. "Oh, here we are on our honeymoon. Oh, Chris! That dear little hostelry in the Welsh mountains! How picturesque it was!"

"You seem to have forgotten that our room happened to be directly above the Bar," Chris reminded me, with a twinkle. He turned to Tony and Cathy. "I'm afraid your mother's memory seems to be slightly blurred through rose-coloured spectacles. We were nearly driven out of our minds every night because the Village Male Voice Choir used to practise right under our bed until about one in the morning. Four part harmony — and sometimes six or seven part when they got a bit carried away on the local brew."

"You thought it was romantic at

10

the time. Like being serenaded," I accused.

"Well, I'm older now. I need to sleep at night," said Chris defensively. He tilted my chin and gave me a kiss. "Poor darling! Am I spoiling all your beautiful memories?"

I shut the Album. "Ah, well. It was a long time ago. Just think — Jill and Robert will be catching their plane for Athens now. I do hope their honeymoon goes off all right. Imagine — the Parthenon by moonlight — ."

"Here she goes again," sighed Tony, who, like Cathy, was sprawled out recovering from too much champagne and too many sausage rolls.

My daughter sat up suddenly, sweeping her long hair out of her eyes.

"Oh, that reminds me, Mum. Our class is going camping this summer. Miss Boscombe is organizing everything. Can I go with them?"

"Camping? Where?" I enquired suspiciously. Cathy was too young, I felt, to go wandering across Europe.

"Oh, not far. The Lake District, I think," she said vaguely. "It isn't settled yet, but she'll be sending you a leaflet about it some time soon."

"The Lake District? H'm. Well, I can't see why not," I agreed, reassured, and she gave me a dazzling smile.

"Dead brill, Mum! I'd love to go camping."

"Rain pouring down and washing your tents away," teased Chris. "Creepy-crawlies getting into your sleeping bag — ."

"Oh, Dad! It won't be a bit like that. Miss Boscombe goes camping every year, and she's been telling us about it. They have sing-songs round the camp fire under the stars — and cook sausages on sticks," Cathy told him reproachfully, and he ruffled her hair.

"I'm only kidding. You go off and enjoy yourself. After all, you're only young once."

"I've got a few plans for the

summer myself, Mum," Tony put in unexpectedly. "The exams'll be over, so a few of us thought we'd celebrate. Go hiking. Stay at Youth Hostels — you know the sort of thing. All muck in together with the washing up, and stuff."

"My goodness! Well, I suppose if you really want to — ," I said rather helplessly. We usually spent our summer holidays all together touring round in the car. Still, I reminded myself, the children were getting older — it was quite natural that they should want to do their own thing. "The house won't seem the same without you two knocking about. Perhaps I'll be able to finish reading *The Brothers Karamazov* at long last."

Chris had a gleam in his eye.

"We'll see about that," he declared, enigmatically, but would say no more, so I forgot all about it — then.

★ ★ ★

Holidays seemed to be very much in the air. The next morning, though it was Sunday, I took advantage of the fine weather to get a load of washing done, and I was out in the garden hanging everything out when I heard a loud "Coo — ee!" from the other side of the fence, and saw Henrietta bearing down on me like a ship in full sail.

I had better explain about Henrietta. I've already mentioned that she is our next-door neighbour. She and her brother James (who is a doctor) had come to live next door the previous summer, and she not only looks like a tank (especially this morning, in a kahki-coloured smock that the Army seemed to have decided was too large for even the most stalwart warrior) but she behaves like one as well.

It was she who had bull-dozed me into appearing in *The Sound of Music* in January, and she'd brought all her guns into play to try and get me to take the part of Laurey in *Oklahoma!*, the Operatic Society's current production. So far, I had managed to resist her, but when I saw her coming, I stiffened my spine and prepared for battle. Fortunately, it wasn't necessary, as her mind was on other matters.

"Ah, Jenni," she boomed. "Beautiful morning, and all that. I just thought I'd let you know that James and I have had an invitation to go to California this summer to see my Cousin Hubert."

"California!" I echoed, impressed. "Oh, how marvellous. You'll be going, of course?"

"Well — James is a doctor, and duty comes first," said Henrietta, with the coy expression of a playful elephant. "But he's fixing up a locum so that we can take a few weeks off, in July and August. Cousin Hubert would be ever so disappointed if we couldn't go. He and I were inseparable as children, you know." She heaved a sentimental sigh. "Then he went to America. Something to do with oil, I believe. He has a most wonderful house in Los Angeles. Swimming pools, tennis courts, the lot. And four cars."

"Four!" I said, taken aback. "Oh — one for his wife, I suppose — ."

"He isn't married," Henrietta said smugly. "Just leads a simple bachelor existence. Only a handful of servants. He's never really gone in for the Jet Set sort of life, even though he's top man in the Company now. No, he's rather a retiring sort of person, like James and myself. As a matter of fact, he and I have always had rather a lot in common."

There was a glint in her eye that I recognized, and to my stunned astonishment, I realized that Henrietta had what our grandmothers would have called 'Hopes' as far as Cousin Hubert was concerned. I didn't know whether to grin at the thought, or feel sorry for the poor man. But surely, if he'd worked his way up in an oil company, he'd be more than a match for Henrietta.

"Well, lucky you," I said non-committally. "You'll by flying, I suppose?"

"To New York, just for us to have a look round," nodded Henrietta. "Then Hubert is sending his private plane for us."

"Private p-plane?" I goggled.

Henrietta smirked. "Well, I think it's a company plane, actually. An executive jet. Just to whip us over to the West Coast."

"Oh, of course," I managed.

"Anyway," Henrietta said briskly. "I just thought I'd let you know that the house will be empty during part of July and August, so perhaps you'd keep a teensy-weensy eye on it for us — take in any parcels that arrive — that sort of thing."

"Oh, of course we will. No trouble at all," I said willingly, and she gave me a smile that revealed all her tombstone teeth.

"I knew I could rely on you, Jenni dear. Well, happy landings!"

"Happy landings," I echoed, and added: "I do hope you have a good time."

"You too," Henrietta gushed, although I noticed that she hadn't even enquired whether we planned to go anywhere.

She rumbled off, probably to pack garments intended to knock Cousin Hubert for six, and I wandered into the house carrying the empty washing basket. Cathy was leaning against the kitchen door, propping up the doorpost. She rolled her eyes.

"God save America!" she said fervently. "They'll never know what hit them. I say, Mum, d'you think she might be able to get Michael Douglas's autograph for me?"

"Certainly not," I declared firmly.

"Well, I can't see why. Los Angeles is practically in Hollywood, isn't it?" Cathy enquired persistently.

"Look, she's going for a quiet family holiday with her Cousin Hubert, not to mingle with the film stars," I informed her, and Cathy rolled her eyes again.

"Swimming pools? *Four* cars? Executive jet? You call that a quiet family holiday Mum?" she queried, then unwound herself from the doorpost. "Oh, well she's welcome to it. I'd far rather go camping in the Lake District."

★ ★ ★

In due course, the leaflet about the camping holiday arrived from Miss Boscombe, and the parents of all the girls who wanted to go were called to a meeting at Cathy's school. Miss Boscombe, an earnest lady in tweeds, who looked as though she really ought to be wearing Fell Boots and carrying a rucksack, launched with great enthusiasm into her plans for visiting the Lake District.

"We shall miss the daffodils, of course," she told us from the rostrum, where she was sitting with her equally earnest companion whom she introduced as Miss Fish. Together, they were to

19

be in charge of the tour. "But we hope to visit Wordsworth's Cottage in Grasmere, and one whole day will be given to a tour by motor launch on Lake Windermere. As you will see from the leaflet, we hope to cover most places of interest."

I came away with my head buzzing with details of what Cathy would need. Tents, sleeping bags and so on, were to be hired by Miss Boscombe, but my darling daughter would want a new anorak, suitable shoes for walking, a rucksack and various other things. The holiday was fixed for the last week in July.

"I just can't wait!" Cathy enthused, as we all sat round drinking cocoa after the meeting, before going to bed.

Tony stretched out his long legs.

"As a matter of fact, that's the week we've decided to go hiking as well, Mum. It'll be okay, won't it?"

"Abandoned!" I exclaimed dramatically. "Chris, d'you hear that? We shall be abandoned!" I grinned at Tony.

"Course it will. What sort of things are *you* going to need? I must get Cathy an anorak and shoes — ."

"Oh, you needn't worry about me," said Tony, carelessly. "I won't need much, and I can buy what I'll want myself."

"But you've never been hiking before. Won't you want — well, a primus stove, and — and a frying pan — ?" I began tentatively, with a vision of Tony loaded down with camping, cooking, sleeping and walking gear swimming dazedly in my head.

"Good heavens! D'you think I'm about to take to the road on an expedition, or something?" demanded Tony. "I told you, we'll be staying at Youth Hostels. All I'll need will be a few clothes and the odd bit of gear. I'm not going climbing Mount Everest, you know, Mum."

"Bet you'll get blisters. Where *are* you going to?" asked Cathy, reaching absently for a chocolate biscuit.

"We thought we'd head for Snowdonia

— see a bit of Welsh Wales," Tony told us, ignoring her remark about the blisters. "And we're planning to travel light. After all, this will be the first time for all of us, and the girls won't be able to carry much with them."

There was a significant pause, then Cathy repeated: "Girls? You mean there'll be girls with you?"

"Of course. I said it would be a group of us from the College," said Tony, raising his eyebrows. "Four girls, if you must know. And five of us chaps." He gave Cathy a mock-serious stare. "We are allowed to mix with the other sex, you know. It might surprise you to hear that they stopped wearing veils quite a few years ago, and came out of purdah."

"I can just see the headlines in the Sunday papers," said Cathy ominously. She flung out an arm and declaimed: " 'Orgy at Snowdonia Youth Hostel! It was the drink and the drugs that did it! I couldn't help myself, said

Tony Fielding, when interviewed by our reporter!' "

"Cathy!" I almost shrieked, while Chris chortled with laughter. "What a thing to say! Your own brother!"

"Well, who knows what he'll get up to once he's away from your apron strings?" asked Cathy darkly.

"I have absolute faith in my son's integrity," I declared, with conviction. Tony's eyes were twinkling, and Chris was still convulsed with laughter.

"It's all right, dear sister. My hookah would be too heavy to carry, so I'm leaving it at home," Tony said smoothly. "I've decided to give opium a rest, and try out another drug instead." He leaned towards her, and whispered dramatically: "The dreaded weed! Tobacco! Yes, I must admit, I do smoke the odd cigarette from time to time. Alas! What a depraved character I am!"

"You're both being very silly," I said firmly. "Tony, don't tease her. I know very well that your friends are all a really nice crowd, and that you'll all behave sensibly. As for you, Cathy, I don't know what Sunday papers you read, but they're certainly not the ones we have in this house."

"No, I sometimes see the others at Anne's," Cathy said smugly. "Honestly, Mum, you'd never believe what some people get up to. There was this fifty-year-old Vicar, for instance, and he and the girl who played the organ for choir practise — ."

"We are not interested in the fifty-year-old Vicar, or the girl who played the organ," I interrupted coldly. "That will be enough, Cathy. Bed!"

When I addressed her in that particular tone of voice, she always knew I meant what I said. Meekly, she put down her mug, murmured "Night, everybody", and trailed off upstairs.

"Well!" I said, astounded at the revelation of my cherished child's worldly activities. "Well, really!"

★ ★ ★

Cathy's end-of-term exams and Tony's 'A' Levels were looming on the horizon, and I spent quite a lot of time during the next few weeks agonizing with them over last-minute revision, and re-living the exam papers in minute detail. Not that I could understand them. I had long ago come to the conclusion that as far as modern education was concerned, I must be a moron. Even Cathy's maths were beyond me, and as for Tony's Computers paper — !

Cathy's birthday fell just after the exams, and as usual, I gave her a party. We all relaxed and made idiots of ourselves with trifles and paper streamers and balloons, although Chris retired to his study, saying that he didn't care whether the music was Heavy rock or Light rock, or even Blackpool rock, he just couldn't stand it. But Cathy and her friends had a good time at our disco, and that was all that mattered to me.

It was round about the time of the party that I suddenly realized that

Chris had been behaving in a very odd way. He'd been throwing out casual remarks like: "You *can* swim, can't you darling?" and "You're not afraid of water, Jenni, are you?" I had answered him without thinking, but now that I had time to ponder on it, I came to the conclusion that my dear husband had some sort of Secret Plan up his sleeve.

Another odd thing was that every time I mentioned the week when the children would be away at the end of July, or enquired when he was intending to take his own holidays, he would mutter some feeble excuse and change the subject, or avoid answering. But it was not until the schools had broken up for the summer and I was busy getting Tony and Cathy ready for their various adventures that enlightenment finally dawned. My husband was planning to surprise me by taking *me* on a holiday too!

Henrietta and James had already departed with a mountain of luggage that rivalled Henrietta herself in bulk. Cathy was eagerly awaiting her trip to the Lake District, and Tony and his friends were spending hours planning routes on their maps. And Chris — bless him! — didn't want to see me left out. Of course! He was secretly making arrangements to take *me* somewhere, too!

I was peeling potatoes at the moment when the great revelation struck, and I stood still, peeler poised, my mouth open. All his casual little remarks about water and being able to swim suggested two things — either he was going to take me on a cruise, or else he was thinking of Venice.

I dismissed a cruise instantly. I knew our finances wouldn't stretch to one. But Venice — and he knew how often I'd said I'd love to see Venice! Oh, the dear! The darling! I felt a sudden surge of unbearable excitement. Chris was going to take me to Venice!

The potatoes lay forlorn as I stood there dreaming. The Grand Canal!

The Piazza! St. Mark's! The Bridge of Sighs! I'd see them all, in glorious Technicolour. Oh, darling, darling Chris!

My mind went reeling wildly on. Gondolas under the stars! Masked balls! Carnival time! I was so thrilled I could hardly stand, and I sank into one of the kitchen chairs, still clutching my potato peeler. Of course, I'd never, never give him the tiniest hint that I'd guessed his secret. I would pretend to be the most surprised person on earth when he finally revealed his plans.

I sat there for quite a long time, lost in a haze of wonder and delight, then I decided that the potatoes could wait for half an hour, and, with some songs from "The Gondoliers" hovering on my lips, I went blithely upstairs to look through my wardrobe and sort out a few pretty dresses and sun-tops that would be just the thing for the sultry Venetian climate. There was one gorgeous sun-dress I'd bought in a moment of madness when I saw it knocked down to a fraction of its original price at a Sale in the town's most exclusive boutique — and even the fraction had nearly ruined my housekeeping for three weeks! It was a French model, and looked absolutely stunning, but so far, I'd never dared to wear it.

But if I was going to Venice — .

I sang lustily as I removed the sundress carefully from its nest of tissue paper, and held it up against me, mentally transferring the background from my bedroom to the Piazza. I'd look like something out of a fashion magazine.

Venice, I thought blissfully. Here I Come!

2

IN spite of my excitement, I was all prepared to put on an elaborate pretence of knowing nothing about Chris' plans, but as things turned out, I didn't have to keep this up for long, because that very evening, he dropped his bombshell. I had just sat down in the living-room after washing the dishes (with Cathy's assistance) when Chris cleared his throat and said: "Er — Jenni, darling" in a tone which indicated he had some vital information to impart.

I looked up. Both Tony and Cathy were in on it, I could tell from the way they were all regarding me with expectant stares, as though I was Dr. Jekell, and they thought I might turn into Mr. Hyde at any moment.

"Yes?" I said innocently.

"Now Jenni, I've been thinking,"

Chris went on, elaborately casually. "I mean — Cathy and Tony are going away for a week in July, so that means the two of us will be free. To — er — do something together, I mean. And you work so hard all the year round, taking care of us, that — well, to put it frankly, I've decided that you could do with a rest too."

"Oh yes?" I said, carelessly, though my heart was pounding like an African war-drum. Here it comes, I thought.

Chris came over and sat down beside me.

"Yes, darling, you need a break," he declared firmly. "You want a change. And I've got — um — a little surprise for you. I've been making arrangements for us both to Get Away From It All and have a Second Honeymoon!"

"Chris!" I exclaimed, genuinely overcome. "What are you saying?"

He put an arm round my shoulders.

"How would you like a week on a narrow boat, floating gently along the canals of Old England? Standing at the tiller watching the scenery drifting past, with just the fresh air and the gentle lapping of water, away from all the traffic and the scurry and the bustle? We'll be able to rediscover peace and tranquillity — re-live the magic of far-off summers." He paused triumphantly. "I've arranged it all, darling. Our boat is called the 'Jolly Roger'. And here are the details."

He slapped down a brochure on the coffee table in front of me, while I sat transfixed, my mouth open and my eyes glazed. Talk about being taken aback! I'd never been so stunned in my life, and it didn't help that Tony and Cathy were watching my reaction with minute interest.

"A narrow boat?" I managed weakly, at last. "You mean we're going to live for a week on a little boat, on a canal?"

"You'll have nothing to do but lie around in your bikini, soaking up the sun, while I see to the steering," said Chris enthusiastically. "I can just imagine it — the little ducks and water-fowl along the canal-side — the green trees passing — . And we'll eat in little canal-side pubs, right in the depths of the country. It'll be just like our first honeymoon, darling, only better."

"If it doesn't rain," put in Cathy, helpfully.

"Or you don't break down," added Tony judiciously.

Well! I had been prepared to be surprised, but this was beyond my wildest dreams. I tried not to think of my Technicolour visions of Venice, and pulled my mind in the direction of reality.

"But Chris," I protested weakly. "I've never been on a boat before. I mean," I added hastily, "I think it's a perfectly lovely idea, but neither of us has a clue what to do or how to make the thing go. What if the engine fails, or — or we break down miles from anywhere?"

"Oh, that's all right. The people at the boat-yard will come out and see to the trouble," Chris assured me cheerfully. "And as for the steering, I'll soon catch onto that. We'll have the spankers whistling through the halyards — ."

"And the bloaters skimming past the wake!" cried Cathy, clapping her hands.

"Heave-ho, my hearties!" contributed Tony. "Batten down the hatches there, and trim her for action!"

"Hand round the grog!" commanded Cathy.

"Yo ho ho and a bottle of rum," sang Chris, attempting a hornpipe.

They were all getting rather rollicking and jolly and carried away, when I enquired tentatively:

"But I thought you needed a lot of people on a boat. I mean — don't canals have locks and things? Will we be able to manage on our own, Chris?"

"Course we will. The chap at the boat-yard's ever so helpful. He said an elderly couple went last year — had the cruise as an anniversary present — and they had an absolutely marvellous time," declared Chris, collapsing into a chair. "We're going to have a wonderful week, my darling. Look — here's a little drawing of our boat — ."

He turned the pages of the brochure, which showed various diagrams of little boats of all shapes and sizes, and eventually put his finger down triumphantly on one particular page.

"Here she is! The 'Jolly Roger'!"

I peered at the neatly drawn little diagram, which was marked with words like 'Cabin', 'Galley' and 'Bunk Berths'.

"I suppose — I mean, is there a loo?" I enquired hesitantly.

"Course. Here is it — loo, sink, shower, heater — the stove will be gas, of course," said Chris, adding proudly: "But the boat's got electric light. All mod. cons., you know." He paused, then queried seriously: "Are you pleased, Jenni?"

"Yes, Mum, are you?" asked Cathy,

anxiously. "We all got together to decide what you'd really like to do, didn't we, Dad? This was my idea."

"I helped too," said Tony.

I looked at their three earnest faces, and heroically summoned a smile, while my last glimpse of Venice faded away before a vision of myself swathed in oilskins in an English down-pour, clutching a very wet tiller.

"Of course I'm pleased!" I declared, putting an arm round Chris, and leaning forward to give Cathy a kiss on the cheek. "It's just what I've always wanted. How clever you all were to think of it."

"Romance will bloom again — after years of drudgery and toil, darling," promised Chris, but we didn't know then how strangely prophetic his words were to turn out to be!

★ ★ ★

It soon began to dawn on me, as we sat in the evenings chatting about the

36

forthcoming holidays, that Chris was really hooked on the idea of our canal venture. He got all boyishly enthusiastic, and kept painting glorious word-pictures of how we'd wake up to hear the birds singing, and watch the sun rising with the smell of bacon and eggs wafting deliciously from the galley.

I discovered that my husband had an unexpected streak of romance and adventure. He even went to a shop that sold sailing gear, and came back with a cap that had 'Skipper' written on it, which he wore jauntily as we sat round the table with our little diagram of the 'Jolly Roger' and a map showing the different canals (which had come with the brochure), trying to plan what route we would take, and where we would go.

"What are you going to do with Sophocles and Electra?" enquired Cathy, one evening, looking up from a book on the Lake District. "You can't leave them here on their own, and you know Naomi said, when she went to America, that they needed the happy surroundings of a family household. You can't, you just can't send them to a cattery or budgie-place, Mum!"

She was looking very distressed, and her distress communicated itself to me.

"Oh, we must take them with us!" I insisted, at once. "We can, can't we, Chris? So long as we keep the cage door shut, they'll be perfectly all right."

Chris held up a reassuring hand.

"Fear not! All is well! Pets are allowed, and I've already arranged to take the birds. I knew you wouldn't want to leave them behind."

"Perhaps you could train Sophocles to sit on your shoulder and squawk 'Pieces of Eight! Pieces of Eight!' " suggested Cathy, poking her finger delicately into the cage for Sophocles to nibble. Encouraged at this attention, he uttered his favourite phrase: "Dead brill!"

"I suppose," I murmured thoughtfully,

38

"that we'll need to take a supply of food with us."

"Provisions," suggested Cathy, straight-faced.

"We can eat in little canal-side pubs, like I told you, darling," Chris assured me, but I wasn't convinced.

"We won't be eating our breakfast in little pubs. And we'll want snacks and things. Anyway, when we park — ."

"Moor, Mum," corrected Cathy, seriously.

"Well, moor, then," I waved such splitting of hairs aside. "There may not be a pub handy. I'd better make a list."

Now, anyone who knows me will tell you that I am a sucker for lists. I make lists of everything, and over the next day or so, I jotted down all the things I thought we might need. When I showed the paper to Chris, he almost exploded.

"Jenni! We're only going for a week, you know. There must be enough here to feed the five thousand."

"We must have a good supply of food in case of emergencies," I argued, and he spluttered:

"But what about this lot? 'Washing-up liquid, medical supplies, radio' — ?"

"Well, they're all things we might want," I said reasonably. "And I don't suppose they'll be provided. But don't you worry. I've got it all organized. I'll get some big cardboard boxes down from the attic for the tinned stuff and equipment — not to mention what Sophocles and Electra will need. What's bothering me is what I'm going to take with me to wear." (My French model sun-dress had reluctantly been replaced in its masses of tissue paper. It was absolutely the sort of thing you could put on to sight-see in Venice, but definitely *not* for a cruise on a narrow boat!)

"Oh, you'll just need a few pairs of jeans and a sweater or sun-top or two. Depends of the weather," Chris said casually. "You don't want to dress up when you're messing about in boats.

Any old stuff will do, Jenni."

But have you ever heard of a female going on any sort of holiday in 'any old stuff'? Jill had arrived a few weeks ago back from Greece with a tan that I could have sworn had come out of a bottle, except that I knew it hadn't; and an ecstatic description of the marvellous time she and Robert had had. She was rapturously happy, and like a true friend, she wanted to make sure that I had a happy holiday too. So she came shopping with me for something special for the boat trip.

I already had a rather nice bikini in shades of green, which suited my fair hair, but on my shopping spree with Jill, I went overboard — metaphorically speaking — and we sat in 'Ye Olde Blacke Catte' afterwards laden with parcels, and grinned at each other like two Cheshire cats as we sipped our coffee and gently eased our aching feet out of our shoes under the table.

"Oh, my, Jenni, just wait till Chris sees those white shorts — and I mean shorts — that we snapped up at 'Suzanne's'," said Jill, chortling.

"And that sailor suntop we found on the bargain rail at 'Female'," I added smugly.

Jill giggled. "It would certainly get the sailors going all right, but not in anyway the Navy would approve of. Shall you dare to wear it?"

"Of course," I said casually, wondering if I would. It made me look like something from a pin-up calendar.

"You're going to look absolutely super. You'll really knock the canals of Old England for six," Jill exclaimed, sipping her coffee.

"Chris thinks an old pair of jeans and a sloppy sweater will do. But then you know what men are like," I said, and she nodded with the knowledgeable air of a bride of some eight weeks. "Wait till he sees my canvas knickerbockers," I added, smugly.

"They'll certainly brighten the eyes of the passers-by. But then shocking pink really is your colour, Jenni — and weren't you lucky to find those rope-soled slip-ons that matched them," declared Jill. She put down her cup. "I do hope it all goes well — as well as our honeymoon did."

Her eyes had gone starry, and I asked: "Are you happy, Jill? Really and truly?"

"Blissfully," she answered. "I know the honeymoon can often be a let-down, but not with us. When you and Chris come back, you must come round one evening and see the flat. We'll have it all really in order then, I should think."

"We'd love to," I said sincerely.

"And as for our honeymoon — oh, Jenni, it was heavenly. I know we'll have our ups and downs — everybody does — but I'll remember those days for ever. The colours and the sunshine — and thinking that I'd got Robert to share it all with. You really must go to Greece one day."

"One day," I said lightly.

Her elfin face with its cap of short

black hair was glowing. "Even Athens wasn't a let-down. The Museum — and the Parthenon — that really must be one of the wonders of the world. We've promised ourselves that we'll go back some day ourselves, but when — ah, well! Now that we're a family we're having to spend on mundane things like wall-paper and paint and extra shelves for my reference books. But I've already sold four articles on Greece, and one day, when I write my best-seller — that's where I'm going to set it — amid the olive groves and the echoes of the ancient gods."

I forgot to mention that Jill is a free-lance journalist. She grinned at me. "Anyway, when you get back, you can give me some material for a few articles or a book set on a narrow boat on the canals."

"If I ever get the hang of working the thing," I muttered darkly. "I can see us going round in circles and getting nowhere, if I'm expected to do any steering." I sighed. "I'll let you into a secret, Jill. I don't really want to go. It was just that the family thought I'd like it — and I couldn't disappoint them — but inside, I'm rather dreading it. Chris is in his element, but narrow boats just aren't *me*, if you know what I mean." I sighed again. "Still, it's only a week. I suppose it'll pass."

She looked at me closely.

"There's something else on your mind, too, isn't there, Jenni? Come on, you don't have to keep up the pretence with me. I'm your pal — and what's a pal for if not to tell your troubles to?"

"Well, I don't really know," I began hesitantly. "What with getting ready for all of us to go off — but Jill, it's the first time Cathy and Tony have ever gone anywhere on their own. It's an odd feeling. Both of them, suddenly wanting to do their own thing. It makes me feel old."

She didn't laugh.

"It happens to every mother, Jenni.

When the fledglings grow up and start to show signs of leaving the nest. I understand. You feel almost as though you're not needed any more."

"Yes, I do," I admitted, seriously.

"But you are, really, you know." Jill leaned over and patted my hand. "You'll always be 'Mum' to them — especially Cathy. However far they wander away, they'll always come back to you sometimes. Let them go cheerfully, don't try and hang on to them. They'll appreciate that, and you know they love you. Yours is never going to be one of those families which gets out of touch."

"And another thing," I went on, glad to be able to talk seriously for once to someone who would understand. "I'm getting the impression that I don't really know my children any more — not Tony, at any rate. He's taken to shutting himself up in his room a lot, and there's a — a sort of expression on his face — he's changed, Jill. It's as though he's got a secret life now, and we've never had secrets from each other before."

She pondered.

"Well, you have to bear in mind, Tony's eighteen, and terribly good-looking. Oh, I know he's never been serious over a girl before, but perhaps now he is — he may be in love, Jenni. After all, people younger than him are married with families of their own. It was bound to happen eventually."

"But he can't get married," I exclaimed in dismay. "He's planning to go on to University — you know that. A wife — and maybe children — it would ruin his career. Oh, Jill — ." My face must have been like the Mask of Tragedy, for she interrupted:

"Now come on, it's not that bad. I didn't say he was planning to get married, but he's a man, Jenni, not a child any more. You have to remember that."

"Yes," I said slowly. "I keep forgetting. To me, they're just my two little ones — my babies. Oh, Jill, why do things change?"

"At least you'll always have Chris — nothing's changed there," she said cheerfully, and the weight on my heart lightened.

"Yes, I'll always have Chris. Thanks for listening, Jill. Everyone always thinks I'm a sort of butterfly type, you know, never a serious thought in my head. But I do feel things very much, even though I might sound flippant most of the time."

"You're a sweet nut who never quite grew up — thank the Lord — and we love you for it," Jill smiled, and I smiled back.

"Well, True Confessions over with, I'd better collect my parcels and go and see about finishing Cathy's packing. Not to mention making dinner for the hungry hordes. Honestly, they'd eat Genghis Khan's army out of house and home. Wait until you have a family!"

Jill's eyes danced.

"If there's any possibility of that, I promise you'll be the first to know," she said demurely, but with a naughty twinkle, as we gathered our bags together and went out of 'Ye Olde Blacke Catte' into the mild summer drizzle.

★ ★ ★

The holidays were almost upon us. Chris took to listening intently to the weather forecast, and muttering hopefully: "The long-range men say it's going to change. We don't want all the fine weather now, and then rain for the last week in July. Keep your fingers crossed, everybody."

Cathy was almost ready to go. Her things were all packed — except for last-minute items like her toothbrush — and Tony too had all his stuff laid out quite neatly (for him) ready to go into his rucksack at the drop of a large-scale map. He was still behaving slightly oddly, but one evening, he came in wearing a fiendish grin.

"Did you say your boat was called the 'Jolly Roger'?" he enquired, with an air of innocence.

"You know very well it is," I replied vaguely. I was just checking that I had enough packets of bird-seed to last Sophocles and Electra for several weeks (in case of emergencies), as well as extra millet. Their things were packed in a separate little box.

Tony pulled something from behind him, like a conjurer with a rabbit.

"Dum-de-de-dum!" he cried, with a flourish. "I've brought you a flag to fly."

And he held up a garish effort with a huge white skull and cross-bones on a black background, and waved it to and fro. I couldn't help it. I collapsed with laughter.

"Oh, Tony, wherever did you get that?"

"From the Joke Shop in town," he admitted. "Like it?"

"Well — ." I exchanged a glance

with Chris, and said heroically: "It's lovely, Tony."

Chris grinned. "We'll fly it everywhere we go. People who pass us won't forget the 'Jolly Roger' in a hurry. It's just great, shipmate."

Tony grinned smugly back. "Well, I just thought you might like to make an impression," he said casually. "Here you are, Dad. Don't forget it when you go."

"As if we would!" said Chris reproachfully. "You — er — didn't get a parrot as well, by any chance, did you?"

"We don't need a parrot! We've got Sophocles and Electra! They'd be most insulted if you took a parrot along too. Not to mention the fact that I don't want a parrot anyway," I cried indignantly.

"Never fear, mother dear," soothed Tony. "There is no parrot. Cross my heart and hope to die. I just happened to see the flag when I passed the Joke Shop, and I couldn't resist it."

"Well, I only hope Cathy doesn't come home past the Pet Shop, that's all," I said ominously.

★ ★ ★

The Big Saturday was upon us! The day of farewells!

Cathy was to leave early in the morning to join her coach party and set off to the Lake District, and in a flurry of last minute instructions and "You'll phone the Main Camp, Mum, won't you, to let me know how you are?", kisses and hugs, she bade me a tremulously excited goodbye after Chris had piled her luggage into the boot of the car. She was thrilled to bits to be going off on her own, but it *was* the first time she had ever left us for a holiday, and I was moved by her unexpected emotion as she clung to me and made sure we'd keep in touch.

"Of course we'll phone. I'll phone you just as soon as I can, to make sure you've got there all right," I reassured her, and she gave me a final hug.

"Have a super time on the boat, Mum. I'll give your love to the Lake District."

"Come on there, or you'll be late," called Chris, from the car, and Cathy gave me a quick kiss.

"Bye Mum. See you next week."

"Goodbye, darling. Have a wonderful time," I called, as she dashed off, and I stood and waved as the car turned out onto the road and disappeared from view.

The first fledgeling to leave the nest, I thought, with a lump in my throat and a curiously lonely sigh. You'd have imagined I wasn't going to see her again for at least six months. I blinked back a tear, told myself firmly not to be sentimental, and went to have a cup of coffee before getting ready for the next departure. Tony and his friends were not early risers like Miss Boscombe, and they had decided to start out at half past ten.

Well, at least it looked as though it was going to be another lovely day, I reflected, casting a glance at the deepening blue of the sky and the hazy early morning sunshine. We'd had several fine days in a row, and were hoping that the weather would last.

★ ★ ★

Chris arrived back before Tony had even got up, and we had another cup of coffee together. He grinned at me.

"All set to sail, darling?"

"Everything," I said sedately, "is packed and ready." We ourselves were to set off after a light lunch to pick up the boat early in the afternoon.

At that moment, Tony wandered in, yawning.

"Aren't you even dressed yet?" I exclaimed, and he rubbed his eyes sleepily.

"Oh, it won't take me a minute to throw on a few clothes, and my gear's all ready. Could you rustle up some

54

eggs and bacon for me, Mum, please? I need to be fortified in case we don't get another meal for a long time."

But it was while I was cooking his breakfast that the accident happened. The first thing I knew was a yell from the hall, followed by muttered oaths, and I dashed through (with a quick glance to make sure the bacon wouldn't burn) to find Chris, grey-faced, sprawled at the foot of the stairs, both hands clutching his ankle.

"Chris! Darling, what happened?" I said incoherently, as Tony appeared at the top of the stairs, asking:

"What's going on?"

"I — caught my foot and — twisted my ankle or something. Don't — think I can walk — ," Chris told us, biting his lip against the pain.

I tried to be calm.

"Tony, your breakfast's almost ready. Just needs putting out. Come down and see to it, will you love? I must phone the doctor."

"Sure thing, Mum. You look after

Dad — I'll fend for myself," my son reassured me, and came swiftly down the stairs in his jeans and string vest to cope with the culinary side of things, while I flew to the phone.

We hadn't had to call the doctor out in ages, but he was there within half an hour — a relief doctor, since this was a Saturday. He strode in through the front door, quietening my gibbering with a calm gesture of a reassuring hand. All six feet of him, and his warm Scottish accent exuded confidence, as I conducted him to where Chris half-sat, half-lay, on the settee in the living-room.

"Now then, laddie, what seems to be the trouble?" he enquired in a tone that brought relief to us all.

While he examined Chris's ankle, Tony and I watched tensely, and at length the doctor proclaimed, in comforting tones:

"Ah weel, nothing much to worry about there. No bones broken. Just a very bad sprain — and you've pulled and torn some ligaments." He turned to me. "Have ye any frozen peas in the fridge, Mrs Fielding?"

"Why — yes, but — ," I floundered, and he interrupted me.

"Better than an ice pack or a cold compress for bringing down the swelling, ye ken. I'll give ye a prescription for an elastic sock — and apart from complete rest, that's all your husband needs."

"Complete rest?" choked Chris. "But — we're going on holiday this afternoon — we've got to collect a boat from the boatyard — we've booked a week on a narrow boat on the canals — it's Jenni's — my wife's treat — ."

Dr. MacTavish looked sympathetic.

"Ye can see for yourself that it's completely out of the question, Mr. Fielding. For a few days, until the ligaments begin to heal, that ankle won't even hold ye up, and as for running about on a narrow boat, working locks and so on — ." He shook his head. "I hope ye're insured against accident?"

Chris bit his lip.

"Well, yes, we are, fortunately, but — ." He turned to me. "Jenni, darling — why on earth did I choose today to do such an idiotic thing as sprain my wretched ankle?"

I went to him at once, and put my arms round him. The poor dear looked so woebegone that I didn't have the heart to tell him that — apart from my concern about his ankle — I was secretly greatly relieved that I hadn't got to spend a week messing about in a narrow boat.

"Never mind, Chris," I told him, cheerfully. "We'll have a nice quiet holiday here at home, and I'll get my sun-tan in the garden in my bikini, instead of on the canals. Don't *worry*! These things can't be helped."

"But you must be so disappointed," he began, and I laid a finger across his lips firmly.

"Not another word. I have all the provisions we need, I shan't have to think about a thing, so we're going to have a lovely peaceful week just doing nothing. We'll laze in the sun — and read — and you're going to rest that ankle if I have to strap you down. I honestly don't mind, darling. At least it didn't happen while we were actually on the boat — that would have been much worse. We can always go on another holiday later."

The doctor cleared his throat.

"H'm. Well, aye," he murmured tactfully, and I turned to see him out of the house. He left me with instructions about the frozen peas, gave me the prescription for the elastic sock, and then, with a nod, left for his car. As I watched him go, Tony said apologetically in my ear:

"Sorry to be a nuisance, Mum, but I'm going to have to go too, if I'm to be there on time. I hate to leave you and Dad like this, but — ."

"Now, don't you start," I said firmly. He was ready, with his rucksack on his back, wearing casual clothes and walking shoes. "Sorry, Tony. In all the mess, I'd forgotten about you. Just let me put the packet of frozen peas on Dad's ankle, and I'll be right with you. Come and say so long to him while I'm getting them out of the fridge. He won't be able to come to the door and see you off."

I slapped the peas round Chris's swollen ankle, while Tony, frowning in concern, muttered: "Well, Dad — I can't say how sorry I am about your trip. But even if I stayed — ."

"You'll go, do you hear me?" roared Chris, glowering ferociously. "You'll go, and have a jolly good time — or else. Right?"

"Right. You're the boss," said Tony, his face clearing. He pressed Chris's shoulder. "Have a nice week, the two of you. I'll keep in touch."

As I went with him to the door, all my maternal instincts came rushing to the surface.

"Be careful, Tony. Don't take any risks — make sure the beds are aired at the Youth Hostels — ."

"Don't speak to any strange men," he grinned, and kissed my cheek. "Don't worry, Mum, I'll be fine." He called back into the living-room. "Bye, Dad. Keep the old flag flying — even if it's only in the garden. We'll put up a flag-pole."

A last quick hug round my shoulders, and my second fledgeling tramped off down the drive, all blond six feet of him.

"Oh dear!" I said worriedly. "I do hope they'll both be all right."

"Course they will," Chris assured me, as Tony disappeared from view, and I shut the door and returned to my invalid. I sat down beside him on the settee and he took my hand. "It's you I'm upset about — having to miss your holiday treat — ."

"I'll wear all my new clothes to sun-bathe in the garden," I told him airily. "And give the neighbours something to talk about. We'll have a delicious, quiet week all to ourselves. And once you can hobble about, I'll get the lounger out for you to sunbathe too. Your poor ankle. It's not too painful, is it?"

"Not if I keep still and the frozen peas do their work," he assured me, and I couldn't help it, I began to laugh.

"Oh, Chris — what a way to start a holiday week — depending on frozen peas! It could only happen to us!"

3

IT wasn't until the evening, what with telephoning the boat-yard, unpacking our cases, and dashing to the shop for more frozen peas for Chris's ankle, as well as fetching the elastic bandage, that I remembered to ring Cathy at her Main Camp. In any case, she would probably have been busy herself during the day, settling in. But after we had had a leisurely holidayish meal, using up some of our provisions (as well as some of the peas, which had by now unfrozen), I sat down in the hall on the telephone seat, and dialled the number Miss Boscombe had given us.

When I had been put through to Cathy, she greeted me in a delighted manner.

"Mum! Oh, dead brill! Where are you ringing from?"

"Well, actually, darling, to cut a long story short — I'm still at home," I told her apologetically, and explained as briefly as I could about Chris's accident.

Cathy was all sympathy.

"Oh, what a shame! The Hand of Fate must have been against you. Shall you mind awfully, having to stay at home?"

I lowered my voice conspiratorially.

"Darling," I said, recalling that the boat holiday had been her idea in the first place, "I'm devastated, but for your father's sake, I'm trying to put up a brave front. He's so guilty about spoiling everything. I keep telling him that it doesn't matter, we can always go again — next year, perhaps."

(By next year, I'd deduced, I might have been able to drop a few hints about Venice).

Cathy coughed, and I said sharply: "What's the matter with your voice? You sound husky. Have you got a sore throat?"

She mumbled: "Well, just a little bit," and I was immediately concerned.

"Don't go sitting round on any damp grass then, or doing anything silly. You may have a cold. Take some asprin right away, promise? As soon as I ring off."

For once, she said nothing about my fussing, but agreed to take some asprin, adding that her neck felt a bit sore, as well.

"But I expect I'll be all right tomorrow," she said, perking up, and I replied fervently:

"I hope so. If you're ill — if there's anything the matter — ."

"Don't worry, Miss Boscombe would let you know," she reassured me.

"What's it like, your camp? And the Lake District?" I asked, to change the subject — more for my own peace of mind than hers — and she raved about the scenery, and the fact that they were going to have a barbeque that evening, and how nice all the other girls were. Apart from the sore throat and sore neck, she seemed to be all set for a good time, and I eventually rang off with a feeling of satisfaction, after a particularly sweet goodbye from her end. Dear little Cathy!

I went in to report to Chris that she seemed to be settling in very well, and from his enforced prison on the settee, he answered:

"Good. At least the kids are enjoying themselves." He paused, then added, with some surprise: "Odd thing, though, I'm quite enjoying having the house to ourselves, too. And did anybody ever tell you, my darling Jenni, that you look about seventeen in those shocking pink canvas what-d'you-call-'ems?"

"I was planning to wear them on the holiday. I put them on for a bit of atmosphere," I grinned demurely, sinking down beside him and putting my arms round him. The resulting half an hour was a delicious beginning to our 'stay-at-home' trip!

★ ★ ★

66

The following day, I set out to establish the holiday atmosphere even more. It was gorgeously sunny, and I put up the loungers on the lawn, and the garden furniture from the shed, and we lay around relaxing, sipping iced fruit juice and reading, talking desultorily every now and then. Chris admitted, as I assisted him to hop in on his good leg for a late supper of salad and ice cream, that he hadn't enjoyed himself so much for a long time. The fine weather seemed as if it would hold, and I looked forward to a lazy week alone with my precious husband, doing nothing, just enjoying his company.

My idyllic vision was to be shattered the next day, however. With no inkling of what was to come, we had gone out again to sunbathe in the back garden (by now, Chris could just about hobble) and I was lying in my bikini, sunglasses shielding my eyes from the hot sunlight, when, about mid-day, Chris lifted his head and said sharply:

"That's the front door bell, Jenni."

"Oh, no! Who on earth can it be? Everyone thinks we're away on holiday," I said, as I scrambled to my feet and slipped on a beach robe of forget-me-not blue. I padded in bare feet through the house, pulling the belt of my robe round my waist, and opened the front door to see — .

"Cathy!" I gasped, in utter amazement.

My daughter, looking pale and wan, was being held up by Miss Boscombe, who informed me briskly:

"We've consulted a doctor. She has glandular fever, so I thought we should bring her home."

"Oh, come in — come in — I'll get her to bed straight away," I gabbled, holding the door open wider. "Have you driven all the way from the Lake District? I'll put some tea on — or coffee — whatever you'd like. And make some sandwiches. How good of you to bring her home." I swept Cathy into my arms, and started up the stairs with her, calling over my shoulder: "Please come in and sit down, Miss Boscombe. I'll be with you in a minute."

"You needn't do a Florence Nightingale, Mum. The doctor said I only had a mild attack," said Cathy, hoarsely. She hugged me though, as I rapidly helped her to change into her nightdress, and tucked her up in bed. "I do feel rather awful, but he said I'll be better in a few days. Oh, what bliss!" She sank back against her pillows with a sigh. "I just want to sleep."

"You have a sleep, then, darling, while I see to Miss Boscombe," I told her, kissing her pale face, and I hurried back down the stairs, to find that Chris had hobbled in from the garden, and was getting Miss Boscombe to explain what had happened.

"Coffee or tea?" I said briskly. "Or an iced drink?"

"I'd be very grateful for a cup of tea," the teacher admitted thankfully, and I dashed into the kitchen to plug in the electric kettle. I made us all some tea — I felt I needed it — and whipped a plate of sandwiches intended for our evening meal out of the fridge. As I removed the plastic film that covered them, and put three plates on the table, the kettle boiled, and within minutes, we were sitting in the shady living-room with Sophocles and Electra chirping in the background, fortifying ourselves.

"The doctor gave her these tablets," said Miss Boscombe, handing over a small vial. "One three times a day. He said that the swelling and soreness of her throat and neck would pass in about two or three days, and she'll be all right, but she needs to rest for about a week. Poor child! She was *so* disappointed to miss the holiday. But perhaps next year — ."

"The story of our lives," I sighed, indicating Chris's ankle and the stick he had started to carry round to hobble along on. "We would have been touring the canals in a narrow boat if my husband hadn't sprained his ankle on

Saturday morning." I turned to Chris. "But wasn't it lucky that we didn't go? With Cathy coming home ill — I dread to think what might have happened. It really must have been the Hand of Fate, as she called it, Chris."

"It does certainly seem to have been all for the best," Chris admitted. "Otherwise poor Cathy would have had nowhere to go."

"And how kind of you to drive her back," I said to Miss Boscombe, who waved a dismissing hand.

"The least I could do. It isn't really that far. I'll make it to the Camp before 'Lights Out' tonight. But I had to bring her home — couldn't do anything else — and at least now I know she's back in safe hands, and she's going to be looked after properly. I wouldn't have been able to rest if we hadn't been able to contact you and deliver her safely into your care."

"We really are grateful," I insisted, but she continued to wave my thanks aside, and, after she had finished her tea and sandwiches, she borrowed the bathroom to refresh herself for her long drive back to the Camp, and within half an hour, had departed, leaving us with poor Cathy.

"All we need now is for Tony to ring up and tell us he's fallen off a mountain in Snowdonia," I said to Chris, as we shut the door behind Miss Boscombe's car. "And he's coming back on a stretcher."

To quote the old saying, many a true word (or nearly true) is spoken in jest!

* * *

My darling daughter was suffering, her face was swollen, and she said she felt like 'death warmed up'. I ministered what comfort I could, and she slept for most of the rest of the day, while I insisted that Chris went back to sunbathe on the lawn, and whenever I could, I joined him, both of us in agreement that his accident had been a blessing in disguise.

What turned up the following day, however, I did not at first regard as a blessing — indeed, my first sight of the character at the front door made me wonder whether he had come to 'mug' us or simply to demand money with menaces! He was about sixteen, with spiky dyed-orange hair, a dangling earring in one ear, and he was wearing tight jeans and a black leather waistcoat studded with what appeared to be chain mail.

"Yes?" I said blankly, having opened the door to his ring at the bell.

"Mrs. Fielding?" The voice, at least, seemed polite enough.

"That's right," I admitted cautiously.

"It's Cathy. I thought she was on holiday, but I saw her in a car going through town yesterday and she looked, well, grotty, if you know what I mean. Is she okay?"

"Are you a — a friend?" I enquired, unable to equate this apparition with my daughter, even at her most extreme, but he nodded, swallowed, and said firmly:

"Yeah. A friend. That's right."

"May I ask your name?" I said cunningly, deciding to be cautious. Would it be wise to let him into the house? I had to see what Cathy's reaction would be first. "You see, Cathy *is* ill, though she's better this morning, but she may be asleep. I'll have to check."

"Tell her it's Grainger," he informed me, and I looked at Chris, who had hobbled into the hall, and was regarding our visitor as though he had just arrived from outer space.

"Oh, well, come in, Grainger. This is Cathy's father. He'll — er — entertain you while I check whether she's awake," I said, and fled, leaving Chris to cope.

I went into Cathy's room, where she was sitting up, much better, reading, and announced in a matter-of-fact tone: "Darling, you have a — a visitor. Someone called Grainger."

To my amazement, Cathy's eyes lit

up and her cheeks flushed a bright pink, though she tried to hide her obvious delight.

"Grainger? Has he really come to see me?"

"Yes, love. But who *is* he?" I asked, taken aback. "He looks — well, to put it bluntly, rather weird. Is he dangerous?"

She gave me a withering glare.

"Sorry," I said meekly. "But he does."

"Of course he's not dangerous. He's just individual," Cathy declared airily. "He's one of the Youth Club gang. I — well, he's never taken much notice of me before." Again her eyes sparkled. "Has he *really* come to see me?"

"Yes. It seems he saw you in Miss Boscombe's car coming through town, and he thought you looked grotty, so he wondered if you were all right," I quoted, straight-faced.

Cathy clasped her hands in radiant happiness.

"Then — he must care. He must,

mustn't he, Mum?"

"Look," I said, wanting to get something clear. "It seems obvious that you're nuts about this lad. Why haven't you ever mentioned him before?"

"Well, I never knew — you see, I thought I was just one of the gang to him. But if he cares enough to come and see me when I'm ill — oh, Mum!" she breathed reverently, and I demanded:

"Shall I let him come up and see you?"

"Oh, *yes*. But — do I look okay? Is my hair all right?"

Her anxiety over her appearance stunned me, and I realised, with some incredulity, that at fourteen, my little Cathy was a woman — a woman who wanted to look pretty for her Man. Well! But, trying to behave as I knew she would have wanted me to, I helped her on with my best bed-jacket, the one with the swansdown border, which I had always considered too precious to wear, brushed out her long hair, and pronounced that she looked divine. As a matter of fact, she did, sitting up in bed with her pink cheeks and radiant eyes.

"But I'm not leaving you alone with him," I warned. "Not in your bedroom."

For, young or not, I had realised by now that I had a potential Romeo and Juliet on my hands, and I thought of all the warnings that appeared everywhere of how young people matured earlier these days. And I didn't — yet — trust Grainger.

Cathy sighed, but nodded, and I went down to bring her visitor up to see her.

I found Chris sitting talking animatedly to Cathy's beau about — of all things — computers. Computers were Tony's subject, but Chris had them in his office, and understood quite a lot about them. Grainger, it appeared, had just taken his 'O' Levels, and hoped to go on to study computers further.

What a revelation, I thought! To look at him, you'd have sworn there wasn't a brain in his head, but apparently he had just taken nine 'O' Levels, and as well as being interested in computers, he played the classical guitar. He and Chris had already made a date for Grainger to bring round some John Williams records for Chris to hear — tapes, rather. I was a little out of date in my thinking, I gathered, when I mentioned records.

"Cathy will see you now," I told him, feeling like the maid in a play. ("The mistress will see you now, Sir!"). Grainger asked Chris to excuse him, went up two notches in my estimation for good manners, and followed me up the stairs. I conducted him to Cathy's room, where she was waiting, looking like a vision amid all that swansdown, and Grainger paused on the threshold and seemed overcome.

But Cathy had a quaint poise, which I noted with some secret amusement — as well as amazement. Was this my little girl? Holding out her hand demurely and saying, with a radiant smile: "Hello, Grainger. It was dead brill of you to come and see me."

"Um," gulped Grainger (again to my secret amusement), and he walked up to the side of the bed as though he was treading on eggs, and touched Cathy's hand as though it might bite him. Where, I wondered, was the self-assured arrogance he had displayed at the front door?

"Want to sit down?" invited Cathy, indicating a chair, and Grainger picked it up, and placed it reverently, before sitting awkwardly on the edge of it. He seemed to have some difficulty in knowing what to do with his arms, and ended up by clasping his hands together and letting them hang self-consciously between his knees.

"Grainger was wondering how you are," I said, tactfully interposing, and Cathy looked at him with shining eyes.

"I'm a lot better, thanks. I had glandular fever at the Camp, and Miss Boscombe had to bring me home in her car."

"You look — ," said Grainger, in a strangled voice, then cleared his throat and tried again. "You look brill, Cathy."

"Oh, Grainger!" Both of them seemed to have forgotten that I was standing in the doorway. "Really?"

"Yeah, really. I thought — when I saw you in that car — you know, all grotty and miserable — that it had got to be something bad. But you — look — ."

His voice trailed away, but their eyes must have spoken, for all of a sudden, he was holding her hand in both his own, and they were gazing adoringly into each other's faces. I waited, touched in spite of myself, by such innocent devotion, (though one half of me was reminding myself of all the grim warnings I had read about young people maturing early). It was impossible, however, to read anything but innocence into Cathy and Grainger's faces, in spite of Grainger's weird get-up. He was really a decent young chap, I thought, moved by their intense absorbtion in each other.

"Oh, Cathy!" Grainger sighed at last, and she responded with:

"Oh, Grainger!"

I had just concluded that they intended to sit and stare at each other for the remainder of the day, when Grainger appeared to pull himself together.

"If you've been ill, you need rest," he told Cathy, in a new tone of possessiveness. "I'll come back and see you tomorrow. Okay?"

"Oh, yes, Grainger. Maybe I'll be up tomorrow. I feel so much better," said Cathy, happily, and, reluctantly, they relinquished each other's hands.

Grainger put the chair back in the corner, while Cathy watched, a look of pure happiness on her face, then her beau declared:

"Well, see you tomorrow, then. And take things easy. Got to look after yourself."

"If *you* say so, Grainger," she agreed,

and he turned to the door, while I made way for him to pass out of the room.

In the hall, he paused at the foot of the stairs, and said to me: "It will be all right if I come tomorrow, won't it, Mrs. Fielding?"

"Yes, of course," I said. Who, after all, was I, to stand in the way of Young Love? (Although I decided there and then to have a straight Mother-Daughter chat with Cathy as soon as possible). I showed him out of the house, he bade me a courteous goodbye, and thanked me for letting him see Cathy (again going up several notches for good manners), and walked away down the drive. I shut the door, and went to the living-room, where Chris was sitting.

"Well?" Chris asked, and I shrugged.

"Our first outbreak of Young Love."

He sighed, and put a comforting arm round my shoulders as I sat down beside him.

"Well, I suppose it had to happen

one day. Cathy is growing up."

"You don't have to remind me that Juliet was only fourteen," I said resignedly. "But I will have a little chat with Cathy."

"He seems a decent young lad, in spite of his appearance," Chris declared, and I gave him a hug.

"Thank goodness for you, my darling. Yes, he does seem a reasonable sort — and I think Cathy's too sensible to do anything silly. But you hear about all these terrible things — drug-taking, and what not, and school-girls getting pregnant — ." I grinned. "But you should have seen them. They just sat and stared at each other, and I think they'd have gone on staring all day, except that Grainger decided Cathy needed rest after her illness. He's coming back to see her tomorrow."

"And the day after, I wouldn't be surprised," Chris said matter-of-factly. "I have a distinct feeling that we're going to see quite a bit of dear Grainger in the next few weeks. Still, if they're here, sitting on the settee watching the TV, at least we'll know they're not out rolling in the hay."

"Oh, merciful heavens!" I said, involuntarily. "What a thought!"

And I went up to have my 'little chat' with Cathy, while I helped her to take off the bed-jacket and get back to being her old self after her visitor.

* * *

I should, of course, have known better. I tried to approach the delicate subject of — hum — well — in a subtle manner, but Cathy simply stared at me, and told me firmly, and with no embarrassment, that she thought she was much too young for any sort of sexual involvement yet, and that if anybody tried anything, they'd soon find out that she knew where to stick her knee!

"Cathy!" I breathed, astounded.

"We had a few lectures on self-defence," she explained, seeing my consternation. "Well, after all, Mum, one's got to know what to do if someone's being a nuisance."

"But what if Grainger — ?" I began tentatively, and her eyes misted over.

"He's not like that," she declared, with utter conviction. "Anyway, Mum, you needn't worry about me. *I* certainly don't want to be one of these silly idiots who get themselves into trouble. How could you ever imagine I'd let you and Dad down? You surely don't think I'm the sort to go in for more than — well, a few kisses — at my age?"

She sounded really hurt, and hastily, I assured her that it had never entered our heads for a moment.

"That sort of thing's not love," Cathy said disgustedly. "It's just plain lust — all sordid. Grainger and I have minds above that sort of thing. You have to get to know a person really well, and respect them, and maybe even get engaged, before you start the sex bit. What we have is much more precious — ."

"Yes, darling?" I said humbly, thinking how ridiculous it was that I, who had been married for twenty years, was sitting here being given advice on sex by my fourteen-year-old daughter.

"Togetherness — and — companionship," Cathy breathed reverently. "And understanding. Grainger would never want to do anything to hurt me."

"But you said he'd hardly taken any notice of you until today," I pointed out, puzzled, and she gave me an impatient sigh.

"Yes, but didn't you hear what he said when he came?"

I tried to recollect the conversation, such as it had been, and came to the conclusion that the two of them had somehow held a long discussion by means of ESP, which I hadn't been able to overhear.

"Well, just so long as we understand each other," I said at last, rather incoherently, and Cathy smiled.

"I do love you, Mum. But you needn't worry about me. Truly." She yawned. "And I do feel tired. I'll have a nap. You and Dad go out and sunbathe for a bit."

And she cuddled contentedly beneath the bedclothes, while I left the room in a rather mixed-up frame of mind. Who, I wondered, had been having a 'little chat' with whom?

★ ★ ★

The weather was still beautiful and summery, I was wearing the clothes I had bought for my holiday-that-never-was, and Chris and I were enjoying some of the 'togetherness' that Cathy thought was so important. And apart from our concern about her illness (which was clearing up quickly) there wasn't a cloud in our lovely blue sky.

Except for Tony.

We hadn't heard from him at all, and I was rather anxious in case he should be lost on the mountains in Snowdonia, or had otherwise somehow mislaid himself. Chris, who had now progressed from hobbling to limping, did his best to reassure me that Tony was probably far too involved with his friends, and that maybe he'd forgotten that I would worry.

"Not Tony," I said, shaking my head firmly. "He knows I'd worry — you all know I worry about you."

But on Wednesday evening, Tony rang. I could tell he was ringing from a call-box, and I told him to give me his number, and I'd ring him back, which he did. The following conversation then ensued.

"Are you all right, Tony?" Breathlessly, from me.

"Course I am, Mum, but listen, would it bother you and Dad very much — you know, with Dad's ankle, and all that, and you wanting a week to yourselves, if I cut my wanderings short and came home?"

"Why? Is something the matter?" I asked in concern, and he hesitated, then said:

"Well, matter of fact, I'd like to

bring a friend with me. You could put someone up for a week or so, couldn't you, Mum?"

There was a strange note in his voice, and I hastened to set his mind at rest.

"Yes, of course, that would be no trouble." The friend could have the camp bed in Tony's room, I decided at once. "But why do you want to come back now, darling? Why not finish your holiday first?"

There was another pause, then he said hastily:

"I can't explain on the phone, Mum, but we'll be home tomorrow. That okay?"

"How will you get home?" I enquired, scenting a mystery, and he replied airily:

"We'll hitch."

"Now Tony," I began, about to warn him against the dangers of hitching lifts with strangers, but he interrupted me, rather impatiently, which wasn't like him.

"Oh, Mum, I'm eighteen, for goodness' sake, so don't preach. I can take care of myself." Then, realising that I was slightly hurt, he added more gently: "I'm sorry, Mum, but there's a lot on my mind at the moment."

"You're not in any trouble, are you?" I asked anxiously, and he was quick to answer:

"No, no trouble at all. Nothing for you to worry about. It's just that — well, you'll know all about it when I see you. Expect us tomorrow. I'll have to go now, there's somebody calling me for supper. Now, you're honestly not to worry. I'm perfectly healthy, and I'm not in any trouble. But — I just want to get back, and then we'll tell you everything."

I was becoming quite disturbed by the whole tone of his remarks, but, telling myself that after all, he *was* eighteen, I managed to reply cheerfully:

"See you tomorrow, then. Just — be careful, Tony."

"I will, Mum. Bye. Love to Dad,"

he said, and the phone clicked off.

I stood with the receiver in my hand for a few seconds, then slowly replaced it. I had a nasty suspicion that Tony had some sort of problem, even though he had said he wasn't in any trouble, and I went into the living-room, where Cathy and Grainger were sitting with their arms twined about each other on the settee, watching TV. Chris looked up, and I reported what had happened.

"Now I'm more worried than ever," I finished, frowning, and he took my hand.

"You can trust Tony, darling. And in any case, you'll know all about it tomorrow."

"Yes, that's what's bothering me," I said. "I'm just wondering what new problem is about to settle on my shoulders."

★ ★ ★

The problem, in fact, knocked not only me but Chris and Cathy as well as

Grainger (who was twined up again with my daughter in front of the TV, in a manner that was becoming somewhat of an every-evening occurrence) into stunned and stupefied shock. I had spent the day hovering between the delights of the garden, where Chris was sitting with Cathy, both of them in agreement that it was hard work recovering from dire and grevious ill health such as that occasioned by glandular fever and torn ligaments, and that a good deal of fresh air and rest was essential, and the front door, where I kept peering out to see whether the prodigal had returned.

"He's got to come a long way, darling," Chris reassured me, after one such foray, and Cathy added:

"He'll let you know when he's here, all right, Mum."

But it was about six o'clock, and we were watching the news, munching cucumber sandwiches to stave away the hunger pangs until I brought in a hearty supper — glandular fever seemed to have increased Cathy's appetite about five hundred per cent, and Grainger, good mannered though he always was, never said no to food — when there was a ring on the front door bell.

I rushed to open it and found, to my incredulous amazement, a young but extremely obvious Mum-to-be standing on the doorstep. She was wearing a sort of loose tunic and frayed jeans, with bands of what looked like rags tied round her waist (or where I presumed her waist normally was) and over her hip-length flowing hair, which was a dirty sort of auburn. Stunned, I raised my gaze to her face, and registered the most beautiful speedwell-blue eyes I had ever seen, and features which were, even in their current grubby state, nothing short of utterly lovely.

But all the same, I had to remind myself, I did not know this girl, however ravishingly beautiful she was.

"Can I help you?" I asked politely and she gave me a smile that was like a ray of sunlight, even though slightly dimmed with weariness.

"You're Tony's Mum. Hi, I'm Rox — it's short for Roxanne, but I hate that."

"Tony?" I almost shrieked. "You know Tony? But how — I mean, what — where — ?"

"Oh, he's with me okay," she said briefly. "Just fetching the rucksacks from the road. We hitched a lift — ever such a sweet man he was, an undertaker but he had the most cheery face — terribly bad for his business, I should think — he brought us the last fifty miles."

I stood there open-mouthed. A pregnant girl, even one with the features of this elfin angel with her impossible eyes, just didn't fit into the picture I had in mind of my darling son's homecoming. But just then, Tony himself came staggering gamely round the corner, and when he saw me, he gave me a big beaming smile.

"Hi, Mum. I see you and Rox have met."

"Well, sort of," I said bewilderedly. "But — Tony, I don't want to seem dumb, but I was under the impression you were coming back with a friend."

"Sure," he said, and turned to the girl. "You're a bit slow catching on, Mum. Rox is the friend I was talking about. Aren't you going to ask her in? We're both ravenous, and she's tired. She could do with an early night."

4

HEROICALLY, I bit back the queries and questions that sprang to my lips as Tony shed the two heavy rucksacks and ushered Rox through the hall and into the living-room. Time enough later to start enquiring delicately into just who Rox might be, and how she happened to have come upon the scene — not to mention what her obvious state of pregnancy had got to do with Tony. I shut my eyes mentally, and said in as bright a tone as I could manage:

"The bathroom's upstairs, — er — Rox, if you'd like to freshen up. And if you're hungry, what about a meal first, then I'll show you — well, somewhere to sleep." (Not, I had already decided, the camp-bed in Tony's room, where I had intended his mythical friend should pass his visit.

In fact, after seeing Rox's condition, I thought she had better have Tony's room, and my son would have to take the camp bed onto the landing.)

I peered at Rox, professional maternal curiosity taking over. After all, she was only a child.

"You do look a bit pale. Do you feel all right? How — um — er — how far off is it?"

"About a month," she said matter-of-factly, giving me a flower-like smile. I could feel myself going all motherly at the knees, but Cathy unwound herself from Grainger's clutches on the settee, and stared interestedly at Rox, then said to Tony:

"Well, good for you. I never thought you'd have had it in you, but you might have waited until you got the ring on her finger. Surely even you know what self-control is, or did your raging lust just knock you over?"

Rox and Tony exchanged glances, then started to laugh.

"She thinks I'm responsible," Tony

guffawed to Chris and me.

"Well, if you'll pardon me for putting my foot down with a firm hand," said Chris, in his 'Now, lets get this sorted out' tone of voice, "I think you'll appreciate that — er — Rox's appearance has come as rather a shock to all of us. Your mother was expecting a male friend to come back with you — and incidentally, you haven't told us yet why you've cut your holiday short. I think we are entitled to some sort of explanation."

"Sure thing, Dad," said Tony, sprawling himself thankfully out in one of the chairs after seating Rox in the other with great care.

"I'll get something to eat," I said, seeing how pinched her face was, and how pale and tired she looked. "Eggs and bacon, Rox? The rest of us are having casserole, but since I didn't know when Tony would be back — ."

She smiled. "Thank you, Tony's Mum. Eggs and bacon sound wicked."

With which I disappeared into the

kitchen and began to grill bacon and fry eggs and make coffee while I metaphorically let the dust settle. If Tony had been the father of this infant-to-be, it would have been bad enough — but since he wasn't, why in heaven's name had he decided to bring a pregnant girl — one who might produce her off-spring at any moment, since you never knew in the last stages, exactly when the baby would make its appearance in the world — why bring her home with him? To stay, he had said, but for how long? And why now, when surely she needed the support of her conspirator-in-crime to prepare for the coming Happy Event? Not to mention her parents, and what they thought of the whole thing.

In fact, after I had served up the eggs and bacon, hastily prepared Tony's room for Rox while they wolfed their meal down, and shown her where the bathroom was and how to get to Tony's door — Tony himself gallantly bringing up the rear with her rucksack and wishing her a fond goodnight before we went down to a family conclave (Grainger by now counted as much family as Sophocles and Electra) I discovered that the truth was even more awful than if Tony had made a confession of paternity.

"But she was there with the rest of us at the Youth Hostel, how could I ignore her?" he asked reasonably, sipping another coffee while the rest of us tucked into casserole. "And how on earth was I to know that her — well, boy-friend or whatever you want to call it — was going to take off and leave her?"

"Well, even if she was left on her own, surely it wasn't your responsibility to take charge of her," said Chris, his brows puckered with worry. "Where are her parents? Her family? Even if the boy-friend did take off, as you put it, somebody could have made sure she got home safely. A loan if she hadn't the money, yes, but — ."

"Dad," Tony said gently, his eye

intense and very blue. "Rox has no home. She's homeless. One of the statistics we hear about on the news. I just wasn't prepared to leave her there, not in her condition. And I couldn't think what else to do except bring her back home."

Chris and I exchanged glances. The thought of that pregnant girl upstairs alone in the world, and the gallantry with which Tony had taken it on himself to care for her in the best way he could brought a lump to my throat. I could see that Chris felt the same, but he said realistically:

"That's all very well, Tony, but when her baby is born, what then? If she has no home, no relatives to turn to and the father has scarpered and left her, we really can't make ourselves responsible for her and a child, with the best will in the world, we simply cannot do it — adopt or foster someone we are not equipped to cope with."

Tony sat up straight.

"I'll marry her," he said simply.

"Bravo," cheered Cathy, turning shining-eyed to Grainger and hugging him. As they twined themselves into a knot of approval, Chris and I tried to recover from Tony's declaration.

"How long have you known Rox — a few days?" I asked in what I hoped was a bracing tone. "Well, give yourself a chance Tony — and give her a chance too. What does she think? Have you asked her to marry you?"

"No," he admitted, and I thanked heaven mentally. It seemed incredible that within an hour, we had been transformed from a (comparatively) ordinary, every-day family sitting round with nothing more on our minds than getting over a sprained ankle and glandular fever, to a sort of melodramatic group concerned mainly with whether Tony would have to marry a strange girl in order to give her and her baby a home. How quickly, I thought, things can change.

"Well, then," I said. "Rox may not want to get married. And I'm sure that the Social Services will be able to provide her with somewhere, even if it's not a luxury home. With a baby, she'll stand a good chance."

In the end, by tactfully avoiding any mention of how Tony's career would suffer if he got married, and keeping the whole thing on a practical level, concerned mainly with what would be best for Rox, we got everyone disentangled and off to bed. At one point, I did see Cathy forming the words, "Do you love her?" in a romantic manner with her lips, but I shooed her up. Grainger, I was glad to see, remained tactfully silent like the gentleman he was, though Tony did give him a few lifted-browed glances. Since Grainger now had half his hair dyed pink and the other half purple, with a swathe of shaven skin across his scalp, and he was attired in his usual leather and studs, with clanking spurs today, I wasn't really surprised, but of course, I told myself, Tony and Grainger didn't know each other yet.

"Well," I said wearily to Chris, as we tumbled into bed, "why on earth did I ask what sort of catastrophe was going to happen to Tony? Chris, honestly, just what are we going to do?"

"You can see the Social Services tomorrow, and they'll take care of Rox," Chris informed me, sounding sleepy.

"But will they? Chris, you don't think Tony will actually marry her?" I asked, after a few moments, but a gentle snore advised me that my husband was already asleep.

* * *

I might have known what to expect, of course. At about three o'clock in the morning, a whirlwind hurled itself into our bedroom, and Tony's voice announced with frantic urgency:

"Mum! It's Rox — the baby's being born, for heaven's sake! What shall we do?"

I sat bolt upright, every nerve alert.

104

Tony's hair was standing on end, and his eyes were vivid with worry.

"How d'you know?" I asked, efficiently, as I climbed out of bed.

"She told me. I heard her moaning and she says she's having pains, bad ones. Sounds like she's in agony," the poor lad reported, practically wringing his hands.

"Go and get the kettle on," I ordered. Whether we were in for a premature birth or a false alarm, that at least would be a helpful action to take. As he dashed off, I went quickly across the landing to Rox, knocking gently on the door before I went in.

One look at her face told me this was no false alarm, but still I couldn't help it, I asked rather feebly:

"How are you feeling, Rox?"

"I'm dying," she groaned. "Or if I'm not dying, I wish I was. Owwwwww." She bit her scream into the pillow.

"But I thought the baby wasn't due for another month," I said, trying to persuade fate to be wrong just this once.

"This month, next month, who knows? What difference does a month make?" she gasped.

"Have you seen a doctor? Which hospital are you booked into?" I asked, prepared to rouse Chris straight away, and she gave a sort of choked laugh.

"You've got to be kidding, Tony's Mum. People like me don't see anybody or get booked into places."

I recollected rather desperately that Rox was one of the statistics we saw on the news, a homeless vagrant with no permanent address, no family doctor or health clinic where she went each week to be checked up, someone who might have wandered the length and breadth of Britain during the months she had been pregnant.

"Well, I don't care, you've got to go to hospital," I said, and rushed across the landing to shake Chris awake.

"Chris, wake up, Rox is having her baby. We've got to get her to hospital,"

I yelled, and he regarded me as though I'd gone mad.

"Having her baby?"

"Yes, now!" I almost screamed. "Here! Chris, you must get the car out and run her to hospital. I'll get her wrapped up and down the stairs. Be quick — quick!"

Outside the door, without waiting for his reaction, I bumped into a rather dazed Cathy.

"Mum, that girl is making an awful noise," she said tentatively, and I informed her.

"That's because she's in labour. Her baby is being born. Get me a blanket or two from the closet, I need to wrap her up for us to get her to the hospital."

Cathy leaped into action, and I went back to Rox. I heard the sound of Chris galloping down the stairs, and the door to the garage opening. In a few minutes, the sound of the car engine rose to our ears.

"Come on, girl," I told Rox. "We're taking you to skilled hands. I want you to sit up and I'll wrap a warm blanket round you once you get down the stairs to the car. In half an hour — ten minutes even, you'll be safe and sound in hospital where the baby can be born properly. That's it — swing your feet out — ."

"I c-c-can't," she sobbed, and I realised in that moment why nurses in hospitals were often dragons who ordered you about without any regard for your feelings — or at least why they often seemed like that. In desperation, I hauled Rox out of bed and into an upright position, just as Cathy came in with the blankets.

"Stand UP!" I yelled — Cathy told me afterwards that she'd never heard me sound so fearsome — and I threw a blanket over Rox's skimpy nightgown and dragged her to the door.

Tony was just coming up the stairs, anxiety all over his features.

"I've put the kettle on, Mum."

"Well, put if off," I snarled, man-handling the sobbing Rox down from the landing. "And then take this girl of yours out to the car. Dad's waiting to drive her to the hospital. Hurry up!"

"Y-er-yes," he said, looking at me as though he'd never seen me clearly before. I didn't think I'd ever seen myself clearly before, either — certainly I was not acting in the usual type of way I would have risen to a crisis. But the sense of power was going to my head, and I continued to bellow out orders until Tony had carried the mother-to-be — very soon now — into the car and installed her on the back seat. He held her in his arms, wrapped in blankets, while Cathy squeezed in beside them, declaring she had no intention of staying behind on her own. She'd even given Grainger a quick phone call while we were transporting the moaning Rox to the car, to fill him in on the situation. I slid in beside Chris, and we were off.

★ ★ ★

109

And yes, it had to happen. We went to the wrong hospital, since we had no idea of the right place to take a maternity emergency — especially in the middle of the night. It was as we were driving across the town to the other that Rox's baby was born with me yelling instructions from the front seat — not that I really knew what to say, but I must have spouted something, Chris said afterwards that I was shrieking non-stop — and Tony and Cathy acting as amateur midwives. When we eventually arrived at the right hospital, Tony's eyes were blazing as though he'd seen a miracle. Cathy, holding the tiny bundle in her arms, was in tears of joy and I felt far more exhausted than Rox, who seemed to have taken it remarkably calmly, all things considered. Chris just said he hoped it wouldn't happen too often, since he thought he'd be feeling the strain when he got up for work tomorrow.

After Rox had been whisked away,

the rest of us sat in the reception place, drinking coffee from the machine, and took stock. What a sight we must have looked, since we were all in our night attire, with either bare feet or slippers. We might have been a group of huddled refugees, but it had been an extremely traumatic event, and we were probably recovering from shock.

As we sat there, the doors opened and in came a figure guaranteed to strike terror into the strongest constitution — Grainger. He headed straight for Cathy, and as she sobbed joyfully against his leather chest, enfolded in his long leather-clad tentacles with their heavy studs, I knew with a lift of my heart, that she'd be all right now. Apparently Grainger had been so disturbed by her account of the goings-on when she'd phoned him, that he decided to come to the hospital himself to give her moral support, even though it was the middle of the night.

"It was so wonderful, Grainger,

you've got no idea," she sobbed joyfully.

"All the same, though," I said briskly, "you know what your father said about having to go through it again. I hope you're not planning a repeat performance, Cathy."

She gave me a withering look.

"Don't be daft, Mum," she said, then continued to sob all over Grainger about what a miraculous experience the whole thing had been.

Tony was sitting dazedly, and I asked:

"Are you all right?"

"Me? Of course, Mum, but — well, did you see the two of them?" (A rhetorical question, I assumed) "How could anyone ever think of leaving Rox and that little girl?" (Another rhetorical question) "And I know I'm not the father, but, well, when you've helped to bring a child into the world, it gives you a sort of right to — to care for that child and protect it, doesn't it?"

"We can think about things like that

112

tomorrow," I said as gently as I could. "After all, we're all a bit shocked and in a state of trauma. When something like this happens, it takes some getting over."

Tony turned to look directly at me.

"I know you're trying to let me down lightly, Mum," he said, with the utmost seriousness. I thought that if he ever looked at Rox the way he was looking at me, with that blue intensity of his gaze, she'd find it very hard to refuse anything he proposed to her. "But I'm not a child any more, and I know what I'm saying. If Rox has no-one — she and the little girl — and she says yes, then I'll marry her."

At this point, I was saved from having to make a profound remark which I had no idea how to formulate, by the advent of a young nurse who asked if we'd like to see Rox before we left, and feeling like troupe of clowns, we followed her through the corridors into a ward where Rox was lying screened off from the other patients. The lights were dimmed, so we murmured goodnight, and promised we'd be along the next day, then we were conducted to the baby nursery, where we waved through a glass window to a tiny form in a crib in the corner — the little girl we had all in our various ways helped to bring into the world that night. Then we went home.

★ ★ ★

"So now what?" breathed Jill, as we sat in 'Ye Olde Blacke Catte' the following morning, drinking our usual coffee. I had phoned Jill to tell her that we were no longer — any of us — vagabonding it across Snowdonia or the Lake District, and that the narrow boat trip had failed to materialise, so we met during our shopping trips as we normally did, and I was able to pour out the tale of Tony's shattering return home with Rox, and the prompt way she had presented us all with a little girl within hours of her arrival.

Jill was fascinated.

"He never will marry her, just like that, will he Jenni?"

"I don't know. As he keeps telling us, he's a free agent," I said darkly. "But even if he does, well, what sort of parents would we be if we refused to accept his wife and child — into the house?"

"But he's only known her for a week, and he's not in love with her, is he?" asked Jill.

"I very much doubt it. I think he's just overcome by stirrings of gallantry and feels he's got to be a 'parfait gentil knight' to a damsel in distress," I replied. "Honestly, though, Jill she is lovely — long auburn hair and the most exquisite features, like a sort of angel by — what's that painter who did cupids — and Venus, rising from the sea — ?"

"Botticelli. H'm, well if she looks like a Botticelli Venus, you could have a few problems," Jill said thoughtfully.

I stirred my coffee.

"In a way, though, I feel much better about the whole thing. Remember me telling you that it was worrying me because Tony seemed to be living some sort of private life on his own, and I felt he was growing away from us?" As Jill nodded, I went on:

"When he arrived back with Rox it was a shock, but the fact that he brought her home, without considering whether we'd take her in or turn her out or what, and that he trusted us enough to share his concern about her with us — well I tell you, Jill, I nearly cried. I was so touched. He really is a man now, but whatever private life he has just doesn't make the slightest bit of difference to the relationship he has with Chris and me."

"Isn't that exactly what I said?" she smiled trying to lighten the highly emotional moment. She added: "And the reason why he did what a lot of youngsters would think twice before doing, was because if he's a 'parfait gentil knight', it's because his mother,

116

bless her heart, has always been a 'parfait gentil lady'. He knew he could rely on you, Jenni, you and Chris."

I swallowed down the lump in my throat. I seemed to be swallowing a great many lumps in the throat this summer.

"They were wonderful, though, Tony and Cathy," I told her. "They delivered the baby entirely on their own, and Cathy never even mentioned fainting at the sight of blood. And she cried all the way to the hospital, and then sobbed how wonderful it had all been all over Grainger when he turned up."

"Grainger?" Jill queried, and I had to explain about Cathy's glandular fever and Grainger's advent onto the scene.

"If you ever see him, you'll be convinced you'll never escape alive," I said. "But he's a grand lad really."

Jill shook her head in wonderment.

"You've all been pretty busy this week then," she commented. "But not having the holidays you'd planned."

"Too right, but the strange thing is,

I feel as though I've got far closer to the children because of what went wrong than if everything had gone right," I said. "I feel as though I understand them a lot better now. Don't things work out in a strange sort of way, Jill?"

"'There are more things in heaven and earth, Mrs Fielding, than are dreamed of in your philosophy'," she misquoted, straight-faced.

"Idiot," I told her, smiling.

"Shakespeare has a lot to answer for," she quipped. "But seriously, what will you do now?"

"About Rox? Well, we're going to see her later today, and we'll have to try and speak to a Social Worker or somebody, to ask what can be done," I said, thinking over the problem. "We'll just have to take it as it comes. But if you get invited to a wedding next week, you'll know Tony asked her and she said yes. I honestly don't know how we'd adjust, but I suppose you can adapt to anything."

5

THE weather was still beautiful and the sun shone genially upon us as we proceeded in a rather more orderly fashion to the hospital to visit Rox that evening.

Everyone went along. Cathy wanted to ask about turning her room into a nursery for the baby, and whether Rox thought the little girl — what on earth was she going to call it, I wondered eagerly — would prefer pictures of Postman Pat on the wall-paper and curtains, or Mutant Hero Turtles.

Chris came along for the ride. He still had to limp a bit, but his ankle was a lot easier, well on the way to recovery, and he said he didn't want to miss out on the fun.

"As I've mentioned, I hope it will never happen again, or at least, not for a long time," he said with a dry look in Cathy's direction. "So I might as well make the most of it while it's going on."

And Tony, much to our conflicting feelings of pride, amusement and horror, was going a-wooing. I warned him that Rox would probably not feel up to proposals, but he said he thought she might feel relieved if she knew her future and that of the little girl — Anne? Karen? Tracy? — had been settled, and she had no need to worry about what she was going to do.

Consequently, he had dressed in his best, put his suit on (which really made this an occasion) and carried a large bouquet of red roses. My heart melted with pride as we made our way through the hospital corridors. How could she refuse him, I asked myself again, even though the prospect of becoming a mother-in-law and grand-mother overnight, as it were, was not one I felt I could just take in my stride. I had plenty of misgivings. What about Tony's university career? Where would they live? What would they do?

But I made myself quash such doubts firmly. It was not for me to interfere in the lives of these two young people. But I did not quite know what to hope for, except that I held Chris's hand and pressed it as we went into the ward, hoping with all my heart that everything would turn out for the best.

Rox looked ravishing, sitting there with her auburn hair (much more auburn since it had obviously been washed) falling round her shoulders like a shining cloak. Her small face was gleaming with further scrubbing (she'd given herself a good clean-up, or somebody had) and the sort of inner radiance new mothers are always supposed to possess. Her eyes turned their incredible speedwell towards us like jewels.

We had agreed to give Tony his chance as soon as possible, so after saying hello and presenting her with the chocolates, fruit and more humble bunches of flowers we had brought,

Chris and Cathy and I withdrew to the waiting room outside the ward itself, and sat down.

"To think, she might be my sister-in-law within only a few minutes — or nearly, anyway," Cathy beamed. I couldn't help a sneaking feeling that Cathy was being rather unrealistic about the whole thing. If Rox and the baby had her room, with or without Postman Pat and the Mutant Hero Turtles, for instance, where did Cathy intend to sleep? I didn't think she'd taken her calculations that far, but we had no spare room.

"So far," said Chris ruminatively, "The one person who has not been consulted about anything, is Rox. It should be enlightening to hear what sort of opinions she holds on all these vitally important topics like what she and the baby are going to do in the future. Maybe now the crisis is over, she'll let us have her views."

At that moment, Tony walked into the waiting room, looking very subdued.

"It's okay, you can go in," he said, without glancing at us.

"She said no?" Chris guessed, and he nodded.

"Just like that. Rox, will you marry me, I asked. And straight away she said: Sorry Tony, I can't."

"Can't!" I exclaimed. "Why can't she?"

He gave me a sideways sort of smile.

"It's the boy-friend, the baby's father. She loves him."

"But he ran out on her, the rat," cried Cathy indignantly. "He left her in the lurch and it was you who saved her. Doesn't she feel grateful for all that?"

"Yes, she's grateful, but she doesn't love me. She still loves Bruce, or whatever his name is," Tony said heavily. "Anyway, I didn't push her. There's plenty of time to talk things over some more. I just came to say you can all go in. I'll sit here for a minute."

Clutching her red roses to her breast,

giving us a slightly shamed glance as we advanced towards her bed, Rox looked more than ever like one of the Venuses by what-was-his-name. I began to reflect that there might be far worse girls I could have been presented with as daughters-in-law, and my feelings of sympathy for Tony's disappointment grew by the minute, as I kissed Rox on the cheek and asked how she — they — was — were.

She indicated the crib on the other side of her bed.

"We're fine," she grinned, and with cooes and exclamations of delight, Cathy and I peered into the crib at the little sleeping figure of 'our' baby.

"Have you decided what you're going to call her yet?" I asked, and she nodded.

"I'd thought it out a long time ago. Sweetpea — Sweetie for short. I just didn't have a chance to say anything last night."

"Oh," I said a bit blankly. "How original."

I had never heard of a baby being called Sweetpea, though I supposed vaguely that it was only the same sort of thing as Daisy or Lily. I reminded myself that everything Rox did seemed to be marked by this same departure from tradition, and I supposed I'd get used to it eventually.

"Bruce and I decided between us," she said, with a flash of bravado. "Sweetpea Jade."

Chris cleared his throat.

"About — er — Bruce," he began, and she interrupted.

"I know what you're going to say, Tony's Dad. But I can't help my feelings, and I love Bruce. I just couldn't marry Tony out of convenience, or because he was sorry for me. I do have a little pride, you know. And besides, it wouldn't be fair to him. He'd be throwing his life away — his career and everything."

"Well, if you don't mind my asking, what are you intending to do instead?" Chris asked seriously. "I understand you have no home, and you can't tramp the roads or live in cardboard city with a young baby."

Rox gave him a long, measured look. I got the distinct impression that she was thinking how naive some people could be, but all she said, very gently, was:

"I'll be all right. You've all been wonderful when I really needed help, and I'll never be able to thank you enough. But you mustn't worry any more about me. I can cope."

"I really think she can, you know," I said to Chris as we were on the way home. "Did you ever get the feeling that you were about six years old, being confronted by an adult who knew all the answers? If I was homeless with a young baby, I'd be frantic, but Rox seems to just take it in her stride. And you have to give her credit for not just latching onto Tony. Although, I think he's feeling it quite deeply, the fact that she refused him."

In fact, Tony plunged dramatically into melancholy. Even though he had originally offered Rox assistance and his services as a husband out of pity and concern for someone in difficulties, his rejection seemed to stir up much deeper feelings. A few days later, when I was feeding Sophocles and Electra and he and I were alone in the living-room, he admitted that he thought he loved Rox.

"She's, well different to any girl I've ever known," he said. "So strong, even though she's so little and fragile and delicate. And I only have to look into her eyes — oh, Mum," and he groaned heart-rendingly. "What am I going to do?"

"Well," I said thoughtfully, trying to think of the right words to say at this important moment, "you won't do yourself or your career any good if you sit about mooning."

"Blow my career," Tony muttered.

"Now, it's no use saying that. If Rox suddenly changed her mind you'd be all activity, you wouldn't be able to get your qualifications quickly enough," I pointed out.

"If," he mumbled, and sighed heavily.

"Tony, don't let this thing get out of proportion," I pleaded, tipping seed into the birds' dish. "You hardly know the girl, and you can't have exchanged more than a few hours of talk with her. But even more important, she loves somebody else. That really ought to be the deciding factor."

He straightened, and glared at me.

"It's quite obvious, mother dear," he said bitingly, "that you have never been in love."

And he stalked out of the living-room.

★ ★ ★

A few afternoons later, Chris and I were relaxing on the loungers in a

128

garden that was beginning to look very scorched in spite of my activities with watering-can and hose-pipe. But the roses were still blooming beautifully, and there was an overpowering and lovely smell of sweet scents. Cathy and Grainger were out, and Tony had taken himself off to moon around somewhere. I was innocently watching the flight of a white butterfly when there was a ring on the door-bell and I got to my feet to answer it. What with one thing and another, I felt as though our holidays were turning out to be busier than when we were supposed to be working ourselves into the ground.

An extremely tall hunk of a young man, dressed in denim with a ruck-sack poised effortlessly on his massive shoulders, practically grabbed me by the scruff of the neck.

"Where's my girl?" he demanded, in a heavy Antipodean accent. "What have you done with Rox?"

"Oh," I gasped, as realisation dawned. "You must be Bruce."

"Don't mess around with me, you conniving sheila," he growled menacingly. "I know she came here, the Youth Hostel told me. With some sneaking limey who had designs on her."

"You are speaking of my son," I said glacially, "who saved your girl when you abandoned her in the middle of nowhere, with nothing. He brought her here to stay temporarily, and it so happened that the same night, her baby was born, so it was quite fortunate that she wasn't on her own, with nobody to take care of her."

"The baby? It's born?" he croaked, rubbing his tongue over lips that suddenly looked very dry.

"Yes, and they're both fine," I said, taking pity on him, he looked so dazed and helpless. "It's a little girl. Sweetpea Jade."

"Sweetpea Jade! Oh my!" he gulped, and sat down suddenly on the front door-step, his rucksack and its various pans and appendages clattering.

"For goodness's sake," I said sharply. "You can't sit here. You'd better come in."

Once in the kitchen, over a cup of coffee, he was able to recover from the shock. It turned out — as he informed Chris and I — that he hadn't left Rox abandoned, he had heard of a job down south, and had left a message with someone who had apparently forgotten to pass it on. He'd dashed down to apply for the job, got it, and the lodgings that went with it, and then gone back to find she had disappeared.

"And they told me who'd taken her away, and where he lived, and — well, here I am," he finished.

I wondered rather guiltily whether it was my duty to offer this new participant in the proceedings, a roof and a bed until such a time as he decided to move on. It appeared that our traumas hadn't ended, but surely, I argued with myself, he was a working man, or very nearly, and

131

seemed eminently capable of supporting himself, if not his girl and their daughter as well. And I didn't think I could cope with an active role in sorting him out, as well as Rox and Sweetpea. Cowardly of me maybe, but we all have our limitations.

Chris, however, saved me from having to make any decision. He said briskly that he supposed Bruce would like to be taken to the hospital, and that Rox, he was sure, would be thrilled to see him.

"Tony offered to marry her, when we thought she was going to be on her own with the baby," he added in an off-hand manner. "But it seems she loves somebody else, and she turned him down."

Bruce, who was already tanned a healthy brown, seemed to flush a sort of brick colour under the tan.

"Thanks," he said, rather ambiguously, picking up his rucksack and bits and pieces. Once more Chris and I clambered into the car to make the journey to the hospital, and we left Bruce to go in alone to see Rox and his little daughter, while we returned home, promising to visit her in the evening.

"Well," I said rather dubiously, as we wended our way home again, "Do you think that's the end of that, or are we going to be lumbered with the whole family? I don't want to be miserable and ungenerous to youngsters in distress, but I can't help feeling I'll be really glad when everything goes back to normal."

"I think Bruce will take care of Rox and the baby, and he'll have the Social Workers at the hospital to help him, as well as being able to offer them both a brand new home in the south," Chris said briskly. "We can just fade into the background now, I imagine."

"What a relief," I breathed. "I don't think I can cope with much more young love, passion and drama. We were never like that, were we Chris?"

He grinned.

"Well, Tony and Cathy were born safely in the hospital, and I never chased across the country trying to find you when you'd run off with another man." He added more soberly: "It's hit Tony hard, all this. I don't think it will be easy for him to get over this last fortnight, and Rox."

"He can concentrate on his career now, and going to University," I said. "It would have been rather terrible if he'd had to give everything up and get some sort of mundane job, just to keep Rox and the baby going, wouldn't it? I can't help feeling things have turned out for the best, after all."

But when Tony came home and heard about the arrival of Bruce and the job in the south and all the rest of the story, later that evening before we went to visit Rox, he took it rather badly.

"You can hardly try to change her mind now about marrying you," I pointed out, genuinely worried at the expression on his face. "They're together again, and it was all a mistake, and she did tell you she loved Bruce even when we all thought he'd left her to fend for herself."

"All is fair in love and war," he told me sweepingly.

"Tony, act your age and stop being melodramatic," Chris said sharply, and Tony turned a furious face towards him.

"It's easy to see," he said sounding almost like an echo of what he had said to me a little earlier, "that you have never been in love, Dad."

★ ★ ★

Cathy thought the whole thing was terribly romantic.

"Just imagine, there he was, dashing off to find her a home, and while he was gone, his message went astray. They might never have rediscovered each other if the Youth Hostel people hadn't happened to have Tony's address. So she might have married him — Tony,

I mean — and the whole course of three lives might have been changed. It doesn't stand thinking about, does it? This is obviously the working of Fate, Mum, and there's no going against Fate."

Fortunately, the fact that Rox now had a home waiting in the south had put a stop to Cathy's plans for changing her room into a nursery with Postman Pat and Hero Turtles, and she now seemed to regard the saga of Rox and Bruce as a sort of glorious fairy tale which, having reached its correct conclusion, was more or less over. Her sudden surge of proprietoriale affection towards Sweetpea Jade faded away as quickly as it had come, and so far as my daughter was concerned, the tale of Rox turned into past history.

Within a few days, Rox herself had turned into past history, since she and the baby left the hospital, escorted by Bruce. They were going to get married, they informed Chris and I proudly, though they seemed rather vague as to where and when the wedding would take place. But they had their house and livelihood in the south, and Rox was already coping remarkably efficiently with Sweetpea, so we felt we had no need to worry unduly.

"That's it, then," Chris said, as we drove home after our last visit. "The end of an era. We really can get back to normal now — if Tony will only stop carrying on like the Muse of Tragedy. Pity he doesn't have a routine to keep to yet, his University work."

For of course, Cathy and Tony were still on holiday, and what was even more inclined to keep us all in holiday mood was the fact that the weather was still blazingly fine. It seemed as though we had had no rain for months, and the reservoirs were getting low. The grass on our lawn grew browner by the minute, and each morning dawned with a glorious blue sky, not a cloud in sight. We might have been on the Riviera.

My spirits began to soar after the

various traumas of the last few weeks. Cathy was well over her glandular fever, and I was certain she regarded the loss of a few days in the Lake District as a small price to pay for Grainger's unexpected declaration of his affection. Tony mooned about with a brow full of gloom, but I told myself that most young men went through a Byronic period at some time or another, and it was nothing to worry about. As Chris had said, he'd forget his blues soon enough when he had the routine and new experiences of University to cope with.

Chris himself was much better. He had been out in the garden relaxing such a lot that he looked like a native with a tan Tarzan might have envied. His ankle, thanks to its constant rest, was improving in leaps and bounds, so to speak, and he could get about quite well now with just a stick to assist him, and the support of the elastic bandage.

And Rox and the baby and Bruce

were all okay too, so what could be better? Even Sophocles and Electra seemed infected by the general gaiety, and trilled their little hearts out.

"What a holiday, though," I said, as we sat in the living-room a few days later, in the cool of the evening. "What a second honeymoon! It couldn't have gone any more wrong, could it Chris?"

He glanced speculatively at me.

"No, it couldn't. You must be very disappointed, darling. Not only to lose your trip on the boat, but to have to cope with an invalid, a pregnant mother complete with baby and a love-sick swain, as well as my foot."

I snuggled up to him.

"I had a lot more time with you as a result, though. All those hours in the garden — the picnic meals — and you couldn't run away from me!"

"You do deserve an extra treat, though," he declared, putting his arm round me. "We won't wait until next year, we'll fix something up now. Another holiday for you.

We've got the insurance money. We could manage something which didn't involve too much walking, for me."

A gleam was beginning to appear in his eye, while inevitably, my thoughts flew to — where else — Venice! He could sit in a gondola and be transported about by grinning gondoliers. He'd only have to limp from the gondola to a cafe table on the Piazza, or up the steps to our hotel. I began to feel really excited. I could get all my finery out again — even the French sun-dress I'd reluctantly had to shelve as hardly suitable for the water-ways of Old England.

"Well, I must admit, it would be nice," I began hesitantly. "And I know just the place I'd like to go to — ."

Chris lifted his hand.

"No, don't say a word. I do have something in mind — something special, different. I know you'll enjoy it. You like living in the past, don't you? And high society — haute cuisine, sparkling wine, all that sort of jazz?"

"The past? High living? Yes, I love it, who wouldn't?" I admitted, in a dazed dream of the ancient churches and palaces of Venice, the antique settings of the five-star hotels.

Chris was looking smug.

"I know exactly the right holiday for you," he declared. "Leave things to me. I'll make a few enquiries."

"Remember you can't walk far," I insisted, trying to underline the idea of Venice in his mind, "You'll have to be transported, either by sedan chair or — um — in a gondola."

"I won't have to walk, you'll see," he said. "Not far, at any rate."

★ ★ ★

"So I'm certain he's thinking of Venice," I enthused to Jill, when we were having our Friday coffee in town. "Where else is there that you don't have to walk?"

"How wonderful if you're going to get your precious holiday at last,"

141

she grinned. "Well, you do deserve it, that's all I can say."

"I've been warbling 'we're called gondolieri' into his ear as obviously as I can," I told her, laughing. "And quoting bits out of a guidebook I've got on Italy. I do hope he takes the hint."

"Why don't you just tell him?" she asked.

"Oh, I wouldn't like to spoil his pleasure. He's so convinced he knows exactly the perfect treat to give me. It was the same when he told me about the narrow boat. I was horrified, really, but I couldn't have let on or it would have upset him terribly. He's so romantic, Jill, he loves to give surprises."

"When is he going to tell you?" Jill asked.

"Oh, whenever he has all the details, I suppose. If I ask when I'm going to be let in on the secret, he looks mysterious and taps his nose, and says I'll know soon enough," I answered.

"So I'll just have to be patient and think of my sun-dress stowed away in all its tissue-paper. I'm dying to wear it. I shall look like some character from 'Dynasty' when I saunter casually across the Piazza dressed in that."

Of course, I should have known better than to imagine I could put a simple little idea like a visit to Venice into Chris's mind. He, needless to say, had had entirely different thoughts at the back of his head — thoughts I would never have guessed in a million years. I discovered the worst that evening, when he sat down with an expression on his face that I knew meant he was about to spring his surprise.

"Well, here we are Jenni darling. Your treat — your second honeymoon — and this time, its going to go right," he announced, slapping a leaflet and some papers down on the table. "We depart on Sunday for a week, and these are our documents and our tickets."

"Oh! Air tickets?" I asked dazedly, and he frowned.

"Air? No, we can drive there. It isn't all that far."

"Oh, it's in England, then," I said, mentally re-packing my sun-dress back into its tissue wraps.

Chris leaned forward.

"How would you like a week at a stately home, where you can take your ease, wine and dine in luxury?" he asked, beaming.

"Sounds all right," I admitted, wondering whether the sun-dress would fit into a stately home. "But what on earth made you choose a holiday like that, just doing nothing in a stately home, Chris? Not that I'm not thrilled at the idea, of course."

"Ah, but we won't be doing nothing," he announced.

"This is a Crime Holiday. We have to take part in various crimes with all the other guests, and solve the mystery. It's a Murder Hunt. You might even be the victim."

144

I was speechless. I have never ever been able to guess who-dun-it when I read a crime novel.

"And what's more, we get two holidays for the price of one, as it were," Chris went on enthusiastically. "I couldn't decide between this one and a Ghost Hunt Week, but apart from being a Murder Hunt, this is also a Ghost Week, because the house is haunted by at least three authenticated spooks!"

6

I HAD only two days — or one and a half — to pack and prepare for my excursion into Murder, and I wasn't exactly helped by the fact that Henrietta and James arrived home on Saturday.

Since we had all intended to be away for the first week of their holiday, I had arranged for the people on the other side to keep an eye on their house, but during the last week, I had resumed responsibility, as it were, and there were a few parcels and large letters to be delivered. Not to mention that Henrietta herself wanted to give me a full account of her trip, and I was only able to prise myself away with a great effort. But if I didn't get the packing done, I would be going Murder-hunting in a bikini and parading up and down the stately home in shorts.

Henrietta looked extremely well, with a tan that gave her the appearance of a West Coast matron. I did detect, however, a slightly less enthusiastic gleam than usual in her eyes behind her flashing spectacles.

"What happened?" I asked sympathetically, and she gave me a jolly laugh.

"Happened? I couldn't even begin to tell you, Jenni dear. Hubert was just as I remembered him, a wonderful host and so generous. He placed his jet, his cars, everything at our disposal. Dear Hubert," and she blinked away a moistening of the eye.

"Oh," I said rather blankly. "Then you had a wonderful time. I expect you'll be seeing — um — Hubert again soon."

Henrietta compressed her lips.

"He did invite us to the wedding," she acknowledged, and I gasped:

"Wedding?"

"He has just become engaged to one of these show-girls, or models or whatever they call themselves nowadays," said Henrietta distastefully. "Naturally, I had to inform him that James is such a busy man we couldn't possibly snatch even a teensy-weensy weekend break for quite some time."

"Oh," I said, "I see."

And of course, I did. Poor Henrietta had been pipped at the post by a young and glamorous rival in the lists for Cousin Hubert's favours. No wonder she was looking rather wilted.

"However," she informed me briskly. "I was only too pleased to do him a favour and bring his niece back to holiday here with us. Nothing special, a simple live-in with a British family, for Kelly to get the feel of the way we live. She's off in a few weeks to college." She turned. "Ah, Kelly, I was just telling Jenni about you, my dear. This is Jenni Fielding, our neighbour — Kelly Carter, Jenni."

I blinked, not twice but several times. Whatever Cousin Hubert was marrying, good-looking women obviously ran in his family. Kelly was a slim, leggy creature with a mane of sun-streaked blonde hair and an engaging smile. The few freckles sprinkled across her pert nose only intensified the perfect bone structure and poise of her face and head.

"Hi, Jenni," she said in a husky contralto.

"Hello Kelly," I responded. "I'm sorry to say that my husband and I are going to be away this week — just as you've arrived — but — ." A wild and audacious plan suddenly dawned even as I was speaking. "I'd like to offer you a firm invitation to come round soon. My daughter and my son will be here all week. And we have two budgies you simply must meet — Sophocles and Electra. They are real little characters, and I'm sure you'll love them."

"Sure thing," she grinned, tossing her mane of hair back eagerly. "I'll do that, Jenni. Thanks a million."

"Don't mention it," I said graciously, turning to Henrietta. "And now I really must go, I have no end of things to finish before we leave tomorrow."

"Where did you say you were going?" Henrietta asked sharply. "Herondale Manor? And what is that, Jenni dear?"

"A stately home," I told her, but a hint of mischief made me add: "I'm to be the victim in a Murder Hunt. And there are three authenticated ghosts living in the house, as well."

Henrietta's eyes bulged even more than usual, but Kelly gurgled:

"Sounds like fun."

"Are you sure this is wise, Jenni?" Henrietta asked anxiously. "I mean, at your age."

"Why not? After all, this is supposed to be our second honeymoon, and we spent the first in a Welsh pub being serenaded until all hours of the morning by a Male Voice Choir," I said flippantly, and turned to go. "I simply must dash, Henrietta. I'll see you."

"Don't get your feet wet," she warned me ominously, and I giggled to myself as I went round to our drive. What getting my feet wet had got to do with being in a Murder Hunt, or even having a second honeymoon. I simply couldn't imagine.

* * *

By now, of course, I had got used to the idea that a Murder Hunt in a stately home would be a far better way of celebrating my second honeymoon than swanning around in Venice, but I did, as a gesture, pack my French sun-dress. Unfortunately, as we started out on Sunday morning to drive to Herondale Manor, the heavens opened and we completed the drive with the windscreen wipers hardly able to keep the gushing water that was cascading down from the car roof under control.

"So much for our summer," Chris said wryly, and I hastened to console him.

"Never mind, we don't need to go out at all."

"Well, part of the attraction of the Manor is the beautiful grounds," he sighed. "Acres of parkland, it says in the brochure."

"We can always go for a walk in the rain," I said gamely. I'd been prepared to suffer in oilskins at the tiller of a narrow boat, and walking in the rain wasn't nearly as bad.

"We could have done that at home," Chris said, sounding dismal. But even he perked up when we arrived at Herondale Manor. Set at the end of a long, straight drive that went on for a mile or so, it was turreted and battlemented and shrouded in creeper. Exactly the place where you'd expect to find a murder being committed, or an authentic ghost.

Inside, when we staggered in out of the rain, suits of armour and crossed banners and swords and maces on the walls provided even more atmosphere.

"I don't think I shall sleep a wink, I'll be waiting for something to float round a corner or down from the ceiling at me," I hissed at Chris.

"The psychic inhabitants are extremely considerate of guests," said the receptionist, a stern lady with iron-grey hair in a bun, a tweed skirt and brogues. "They do not manifest themselves during the night hours."

"When — er — when do they appear, then?" I dared to ask this fearsome-looking female, and she gave me a look over the tops of her spectacles.

"We can never tell in advance when one of them is going to manifest itself, Mrs Fielding, except that they always do it during the day."

"What do they look like?" Chris enquired, and Miss Dracula bared her fangs at him.

"If I told you, that would be spoiling the fun, wouldn't it?" she teased, with horrible glee, and he looked a bit startled, but agreed:

"Yes, I suppose it would."

"You are in Room 12, at the top of the Grand Staircase," went on the Ape-woman, handing him a large key that looked as though it belonged in some ancient dungeon. "Your bags will be brought up. Tea is now being served in the Great Hall, and dinner will be at seven-thirty in the Dining Room, after which guests will gather in the Hall to be briefed on the Murder."

"Thank you," Chris said, straight-faced, and we began to mount the Grand Staircase to our room.

"Well, I have to admit, it was certainly an experience," I told Tony and Cathy (and Grainger, of course) once we were safely back home, and things had settled down. "You should have seen our room, shouldn't they Chris. It was draped from ceiling to floor in things like damask and brocade — at least, I'm assuming that's what they were. And we had a four-poster bed and a mediaeval chest studded with nails, which we could both have got lost in without any trouble. I suppose it was wonderful really, if you like that sort of thing."

"But did you see any ghosts?" Cathy

demanded eagerly. "What sort of ghosts were they?"

Chris and I glanced at each other.

"Well, we've been arguing about this all week," I began, and Chris interrupted:

"Your mother ate too much roast duckling on our first evening, and she swore she saw a Green Archer standing on the stairs as we were going up to bed later."

"I did," I said indignantly. "Bright green. And he was carrying a bow and arrow, and pointing it at us."

"Dead brill!" breathed Cathy, eyes wide.

"Except that it wasn't there," Chris scoffed affectionately. "You know how suggestible your mother is, people. Why do you think Miss Dracula at the Reception Desk would never tell anybody what the ghosts were ghosts of? So that nobody knew exactly what they were looking out for. Out of the guests who were with us this week, Miss Drew thinks she saw a Grey

Lady, carrying her head, Mr and Mrs Thorpe swear they saw and heard a knight in armour, clanking chains after him, and apart from your mother and her Green Archer, some of the others said they encountered a monk, a nun, a ghostly carriage with headless horses and a grieving maiden, wringing her hands. And those are the ones we heard about."

"Oh, what a shame," cried Cathy. "So you think the Manor wasn't really haunted after all?"

Chris gave a twinkle.

"I didn't say that. I was sitting in the conservatory resting my ankle, when I saw a perfectly ordinary little man come in with a watering-can, and start watering some of the flowers," he said mysteriously. "And then, he just walked through the wall and disappeared. I wondered where he'd gone for about half an hour after, until it dawned on me that I'd seen one of the real ghosts of the Manor."

"Well anyway, nobody could say that

they didn't see something," I added. "I was terrified all the time, for the first day or two, I kept expecting a spook to just pop out from somewhere. But then I got used to it. And after all, we were more worried later about the murder."

"How do you mean, worried about the murder?" Tony asked flippantly.

"Well, they said it could happen any time, even at night," I explained. "And nobody knew who was going to get murdered."

"Charming," Tony commented, lifting an eyebrow and folding his arms. "But hardly ideal for a second honeymoon, I should think."

I reflected for a moment, while I sipped the coffee I was drinking and reached for a sandwich from the plate on the table.

"All told, we spent most of the time apart," I said. "Since Chris couldn't walk much, he sat in the conservatory and admired the flowers — he liked it there — and I went round with a

Frenchman called Jean-Paul, who was blond and quite devastating, searching for clues."

Cathy was goggling, and so were Tony and Grainger.

"You mean you let her, Dad?" Cathy asked in a tone of disbelief.

Chris grinned, and blew me a kiss from across the room.

"I asked him to partner her, actually. Otherwise she'd have been stuck with one of the weirdies who kept wandering in and out in rope-soled sandals and shorts, with earnest round glasses and thinning ginger hair. I couldn't have condemned the poor darling to a week of that, now could I?"

"But this Frenchman — I mean, you know what Frenchmen are like," Cathy hinted darkly, and Chris turned to me, all innocence.

"What *was* he like, darling?"

"A perfect gentleman," I said, rather glumly. Even the moonlight in the Long Gallery, when I was wearing a silver dress that gave the illusion of cobwebs (or at any rate, I kidded myself that it did) had not tempted Jean-Paul to the slightest hint of an indiscretion. His mind had been entirely occupied with the clues of the Murder Hunt.

What had actually provided my most romantic moment was when I had been selected — much as Chris had predicted — to be the victim, and I had had to take part in a pre-arranged scene where I was 'found murdered' by all the other guests as they emerged into the Great Hall after dinner. In keeping with the theatrical idea, I had decided to give my French sun-dress its first airing, even though outside, it was still pouring with rain, and I was lying draped dramatically on the skin rug before the enormous fireplace, a dagger looking as though it was stuck in my back (Miss Dracula had arranged everything) when Chris, along with the other guests, came unsuspectingly onto the scene.

It still made me tingle, even days later, to think of how Chris had run — actually run forward, his bad ankle miraculously holding him up, and swept me into his arms, declaiming tragically:

"Oh, my darling, my beautiful, my love, Jenni!"

It hadn't even spoiled the moment of glory for me when Miss Dracula immediately told him off in a very loud voice because he had touched the victim, and spoiled the effect of the dagger, which was supposed to give everybody a lot of clues. I knew I would never forget his voice nor the closeness of his embrace when he thought I had been foully done in, for as long as I lived — and for that alone, I would have informed anybody who had asked me that as second honeymoons go, ours had been a fantastic success.

★ ★ ★

Mind you, it wasn't quite as simple as it should have been, just a week spent hunting ghosts and hunting clues. Traumas, as will be obvious, follow us around, and a very human and unexpected trauma turned up on Wednesday evening, when Chris and I were having a late coffee in the conservatory.

We were agreeing that events seemed to be going very well, all things considered, and wondering how the children were coping at home, when a familiar figure suddenly pushed its way through the potted palms and held out its hand to me in a very dramatic manner.

"Jill!" I exclaimed, in surprise. "I didn't know you were going to be here."

"I've left him!" she said tearfully. It was very disturbing to see the sensible and self-possessed Jill quivering on the verge of hysterics, and I took her hand and pulled her to sit down beside me.

"Now, what on earth's happened?" I asked, chafing her hand encouragingly. She was cold, and she also seemed rather wet. "Have you just arrived, now?" I queried. "Did you drive here?"

She nodded.

"I had to come and talk to you. I couldn't think where else to go, and I just couldn't have stayed there another minute with that — that — ." Words obviously failed her.

"Robert? Surely not Robert?" I asked incredulously.

"Don't mention his name to me," she hissed, glaring. "I never want to hear it again."

"But what has he done?" I asked, rather weakly. Chris had obviously decided that silence was the better part of discretion, and was carefully saying nothing.

Jill fumbled in her bag for her handkerchief and began to mop her eyes.

"Oh, Jenni, I'm so miserable," she moaned. "It was all a terrible mistake, I should never have married him, I might have known it wouldn't work out. I should have realised what he was like."

"But Jill," I asked, my concern increasing by the minute. "Just tell me what he's done. Attacked you? Gone off with another woman — ."

"If that was all," Jill flashed contemptously, and I glanced at Chris.

"I'll go and order some more coffee," he said, rising with a bit of an effort to his feet and limping out so that Jill and I were alone.

"Now then. Come on, you can tell a pal. What are pals for?" I said encouragingly, and Jill clasped both my hands.

"He read a new short story I'd written, very dramatic, about a woman who loses her son," she confessed, her lips trembling. "And at the end, he — he *laughed*! Said I was being childish and melodramatic."

"And was that all?" I asked, bewildered.

"Isn't it enough?" Jill threw back. "As a matter of fact, it isn't all, either. He complains when I squeeze the toothpaste in the middle of the

163

tube, and goes round tidying up after me and driving me insane. Oh, Jenni — ." And she gulped piteously. "I'm so utterly miserable. I just don't know what to do."

"Well, I'll tell you what you're going to do," I said bracingly. "First, when Chris brings the coffee, you're going to drink it and just sit quiet. Then — did you book in at the Manor, or what? Or were you planning to go back home?"

"Never, ever again!" she declared. "I'll book in, that's if I won't be spoiling your fun. But this is a hotel isn't it, and I've got to sleep somewhere."

"No problem. I think they have rooms, but we can check in a little while," I encouraged. "And you're to get a good night's sleep and then I'm sure you'll see things differently. I hate to say it, but you know everybody goes through this."

"They can't possibly," cried Jill. "They're not married to — that pig!"

"Well, I went through it," I told her, and she stared unbelievingly.

"You? But you love Chris."

"Of course I do. The same way you love Robert — and give me a chance to speak before you shoot me down in flames," I said, lifting a hand to shut her up. "It's well known that love and hate run very close — you should be telling me all this, Jill, not me telling you, since you're the writer — but you can really love someone to death one minute, and the next you can hate them so much you could kill them."

"Psychologically sound, of course, though not very clinically expressed," she said, with a rather watery smile, wiping her eyes.

"Well, with me and Chris, it was when I got a new dress, and I did myself up to look really stunning one evening when he was taking me out — this was before the children were born. I put my hair up, and the dress was one of those slinky sheath things people wore then, with a plunging neckline and slit skirt. And I'd bought new earrings as well, all fake glam and glitter," I grinned. "And I got ready and paraded out of the bedroom all set to knock him over. And guess what he did?"

"Don't tell me," said Jill, a hand at her mouth, where in spite of herself, her amusement was beginning to make her mouth twitch.

"Yep — he laughed," I told her. "So you're not the only one, kid. And I did just the same as you. I stormed out in my too-high heels, and tottered down the road with a suitcase and went home to mother. At least, it was to his mother — my own mother was dead."

"And what did she say?" Jill asked, beginning to relax a little.

"Well, his mother is a great character, as you know Jill. She devotes her life to Worthy Causes, and never pays much attention to the ordinary, normal creatures in the world who don't need assisting. When I turned up, she was overseeing one of her starving stray cats having her kittens, and she didn't even

166

listen when I tried to pour everything out. She told me to be quiet — "You're disturbing Fluff," she said. "And I want this to be a wonderful experience for her. At last she can have her kittens safely, without worrying whether she can feed them or give them shelter. This is the first time in her life she's been secure, really secure."

"Oh!" breathed Jill.

"Yes, that was exactly how I felt," I admitted. "I ended up feeling so grateful for all my blessings that before Mother had even got round to asking why I was there, or doing more than yell at me to fetch her this, or bring that, or answer the phone from the WVS or the St John Ambulance Brigade, I'd gone back home to Chris. And I just threw my arms round him and hugged him and cried all over him."

"Well, that's as maybe, but I'm not prepared to go and cry all over Robert. I want an apology," Jill said. "I have my pride, Jenni."

"Chris used to tell me off for splodging

the toothpaste in the middle. He still does," I offered, as encouragement.

"If he'll meet me halfway," she said consideringly. "I'd be ready to accept that."

"We'll have to see what can be done," I said, and turned as Chris advanced towards us, followed by a waiter carrying a tray of coffee. "Ah, the coffee. I'm sure you're ready for this, Jill."

* * *

So in a way, we spent part of our second honeymoon alongside Jill's first, or at least, alongside the squabbles that inevitably happen in those early, ecstatic months when feelings can run high. There was no problem over booking her a room in the hotel (the ordinary part, not the Murder Hunt and Ghost Week, of course) and the next morning she joined Chris and me for a leisurely breakfast.

We sat at a table in an alcove,

where an enormous French window revealed the most wonderful vista of the parkland Chris had mentioned. It was a bit wet and drippy, since the rain had still not stopped, but magnificent all the same, and so was the breakfast. All the food at the Manor was superb, and I was revelling in some sort of exotic marmalade that appeared to have every fruit from Kiwi to Passion in it, when Jill sat down.

"Feel better this morning?" I asked brightly, and she nodded.

"Yes, I did manage to sleep. My bed was very comfortable." She looked down at her plate and bit her lip. "I do feel a fool, Jenni, but I'm just not going to go crawling back with my tail between my legs, and lick his hand. I'm an independent woman, I have a career in which I'm quite successful — some people might even say more than quite. And I won't have it dismissed as though it's just some sort of piddling hobby."

By now, her cheeks were red and her

eyes were shooting sparks.

"He didn't mean it like that, I'm sure," I hastened to explain. "He was laughing with you, fondly, not at you."

"It didn't sound like that to me," Jill said in a frosty tone. "And neither did the part about me being childish."

"Oh, Jill, you're over-reacting," I said distressed, as I poured her some orange juice. "But if that's how you feel, there we are, there's nothing I can say. What will you do today, go back?"

"No," she said coolly. "I'll stay here. I can sit in the lounge and read — I need a break, I'd been working hard on that story."

"Did you let him know where you were going?" Chris asked and she shook her head.

"Well, don't you think he might worry?" my husband pursued gently.

"Let him," snapped Jill. "I'm worried, so why shouldn't he be?" And she rose from the table and left us, sniffling ominously.

170

"Oh, poor Jill!" I exclaimed, but when I looked at Chris, he was — surely he couldn't be, but he was — smiling! "You unfeeling pig," I added. "Heartless male chauvinist, pleased to see her in tears."

"Give her a day," he said, with an airy wave of his hand. "She may hate life with him, but she'll hate it far more without him. By tonight, she'll be on her way back, you'll see."

"You," I said cuttingly, "are nothing but a brute!"

And I too rose and left him.

★ ★ ★

Jill and I spent the morning trying to decide on the best sort of torture for men, and how it should be applied. Robert couldn't contact Jill, of course, since he had no idea where she was, and Chris made no effort to follow me round with an apology. Both of us simmered like kettles which had just reached the boil, and both of us felt utterly miserable.

"I'd never have thought it of Chris," I said. "He's the last person I'd have said would be unsympathetic. But he doesn't even care about me, he hasn't bothered to come and say sorry — or even to say anything."

"Men just aren't worth it," Jill concluded darkly. "You waste the best years of your life on them, and what do you get back? A kick in the teeth!"

"He knows I'm bound to be here somewhere, and it would be easy to find me," I pursued. "And his ankle's not that bad now. He could at least make the effort. I bet he wasn't bothered that I walked out on him. And this is supposed to be our second honeymoon. I can draw only one conclusion, Jill — he just doesn't care."

"If Robert had cared, would he have laughed at my work?" she demanded. "Would he have said I was childish?"

"I never quarrel with Chris," I confessed, on the verge of tears. "Oh, Jill, I feel rotten. And it's all his fault."

"And I feel rotten," she told me, equally tearful. "And it's all his."

"Why don't you tell him how rotten you feel?" I suggested. "Phone him up and tell him what a — a — ."

"Brute?" she said.

"Yes, what a brute he is to make you feel so bad. And I'll tell Chris what a brute he is — except," I added, suddenly remembering, "that I've already told him."

"It does no good," Jill said gloomily.

"Well, try. I'll tell Robert what a pig he's been to you, if you like," I offered.

"No, he's my pig, I'll tell him," Jill retorted with spirit.

So we made a phone call to Robert's office — he worked in a bank, but Jill said she just didn't care what anybody thought about him receiving personal calls during the day, this was an emergency. We were told, however, that Mr Durham was not at work that day, as he was ill.

"Ill?" Jill went two tones paler as

she put the phone down. "He's ill? Oh, Jenni, if he's ill and I've been the cause of it, I'll never forgive myself. He could have been more upset than he let on — he might have lain awake all night, crying — he could have, well, contemplated doing something drastic — Oh!" Her hands flew to her cheeks in distress. "Oh, Jenni, I must go to him straight away."

"It could all be a cunning plot," I said. "Maybe he's not ill at all. He might be trying to con you."

She looked me straight in the eye.

"If the receptionist came over and told you Chris was ill, would you stop to consider whether it was a con — or would you go?"

"You're right," I said heavily. "Well, have you much packing to do?"

"No, I only have my overnight bag, I'll check out straight away and I should be home by three. Oh, how could I have taken it to heart so much, been so proud that pride came before what I really feel for him? I love him to distraction, Jenni, that was why I was so hurt when he laughed. All writers are vulnerable about their work, he ought to know that. But nothing matters any more, not even my wretched story, so long as Robert is all right."

* * *

"So she went scuttling back with her tale between her legs, all ready to lick his hand?" teased Chris, and I said severely:

"There is a nasty streak in you, you know. And how are you so sure she went anywhere?"

I had just joined him for lunch. We had arrived at our table at the same time after the gong went and I hadn't been able to resist the fact that Chris was smiling his familiar, crooked smile at me, the one that made his eyes twinkle the same vivid blue as Tony's.

"Have you had a good morning?" I asked him formally, and he responded:

"Excellent, thank you. And you? And Jill, of course?"

"Wonderful," I lied heartily.

And that was when he made his nasty remark about Jill scuttling back with her tail between her legs.

"For all you know," I told him, "she might simply have decided to have lunch in the Gingham Restaurant or the Bar instead of here with us."

"Ah, but she didn't," he grinned. "She went home, just like I said she would. Just like I told Robert she would."

I was almost speechless for a minute, then I managed to gasp out:

"Just like you told Robert? You mean you and Robert — ?"

"I phoned him as soon as you two took yourselves off," he informed me. "Suggested that if the two of you decided to try and contact him at the bank, he might be unavailable. It worked, I take it?"

"Well, honestly, of all the under-handed — !" I exploded, and he grinned even more.

"She went, though, didn't she?"

"You mean he never was ill? He didn't care at all about what she felt like?"

"Of course he cared," Chris said, suddenly serious. "But men and women respond differently. She flew off the handle at a fond, genuine comment — and if she can't take criticism yet, she's got a lot to learn, wouldn't you say? And he felt she'd got to be the one to climb down off her high horse. But when she gets back, they can sort all that sort of thing out in the far distant future. There's nothing less likely to quench passion than a lot of introspection and psychological analysis. I bet they just hug each other, and that'll say a lot more than all the words in the world."

I was silent for a while, as we ate. Then I said:

"I'm awfully glad I'm married to you, you know."

And in the afternoon, he rested his

ankle in the conservatory, while I went off with Jean-Paul to look for clues.

★ ★ ★

It was rather difficult to say who won the Murder Hunt, as nobody solved the crime, but I think I can claim I played a starring role (similar to Maria in 'The Sound of Music', which I had played on the stage) as the victim. I was photographed in my gorgeous sun-dress, lying on the skin rug in the Great Hall, stabbed by my dagger, as well as standing on the terrace during the one half-hour that the sun came out in the course of the whole week. The pictures appeared in the local paper, and also in the new brochure that Herondale Manor was preparing to promote the Murder Hunt holiday. And I was presented with a special little trophy which looked rather like an Oscar, and had written on it 'Awarded to Jenni Fielding as a Perfect Victim,' at the ceremony on our last evening.

Chris had a little trophy that said he had used the most intuitive methods of detection, and Jean-Paul had one that said he had collected the most clues, so we were all pleased. Miss Drew had one for the most sightings of a ghost (she had seen the Grey Lady fifteen times in the course of the week!) and another guest whose name I never heard got one for seeing the most interesting spook. He had apparently sighted an Oriental Goddess with six arms, sitting half-way up the stairs.

As we loaded our cases into the car and drove away on Saturday morning, the clouds lifted, the rain stopped and the sun began to shine. And our thoughts turned to what we would find awaiting us at home.

Jill had phoned me to say wasn't marriage wonderful, and the great thing about having a quarrel was the making-up, which I found an exceeding trite remark coming from a writer, but I concluded that she was too happy to try and be clever, and was using the easiest cliches that came to hand to express her feelings. At any rate, things were well in the Durham household.

"I'm sure Tony and Cathy will have managed perfectly all right," Chris said, as I turned my thoughts to our own little domain, and regretted leaving my two chickens to cope on their own all week.

"I'll never forgive myself if anything's happened to them or to Sophocles and Electra," I mourned.

"Hardly likely we'd have got this far without knowing about it, if such a traumatic event has occurred, as they had only to pick up the phone and tell us about it," Chris pointed out drily. "Don't worry, Jenni. Everything will be quite all right."

And of course, it was. The house was still standing, the birds were still in their cage, looking as bright-eyed and healthy as ever, Cathy, who would at one time have thrown herself into my arms in welcome, now gave me a casual wave from her twined-up position on the settee with Grainger and said: "Hi, Mum." Tony was noticeable by his absence, and was out when we arrived back.

"And Mum, you'll never guess what he's doing, who he's out with," Cathy sparkled, her whole being alight.

"Oh, I think I've got a good idea," I said, chortling quietly to myself. Chris, however, looked mystified.

"Is he still mooning around over Rox? Don't tell me he's travelled down south to see her!" There was real alarm in his voice.

Cathy laughed.

"You're way behind the times, Dad. You see, when Henrietta came back from the good old U.S. of A, she and her brother brought Cousin Hubert's niece — or great-niece — or something — back to stay with them."

"Yes, I know. I met her," I said, elaborately casual. "Kelly Carter, I believe her name is. A charming girl. Matter of fact, I invited her to come across — I told her your father and

I would be away, but I explained my son and daughter would be available to entertain her."

"Good for you, Mum," gurgled Cathy, delightedly. "Entertain her is the word. Tony was mooning around looking like he was at death's door — like he has been, you know — when she knocked and explained who she was. Well, talk about love at first sight — I don't know if that's what it is, but he went all goofy at the edges, and ever since, he's never left her side. It's been positively embarrassing, hasn't it Grainger?"

"Yeh," Grainger agreed noncommittally.

Chris twinkled at me.

"You little fiend," he teased. "That's what you were hoping for, wasn't it? A happy ending for everyone."

"Well, I did have some sort of plan in mind to this effect," I agreed sedately. "But we've let ourselves in for a real headache now — what are we going to do with Tony when Kelly has to go back to America?"

For a moment there was a non-plussed silence, then Grainger cleared his throat.

"Well, I've got this cousin — ," he began helpfully.

THE END

Six people get together ———
of their own, and the result is one
of misunderstanding, suspicion and
mounting tension.

THE WISDOM OF LOVE
Janey Blair

Barbie meets Louis and receives
flattering proposals, but her reawak-
ened affection for Jonah develops
into an overwhelming passion.

MIRAGE IN THE MOONLIGHT
Mandy Brown

En route to an island to be secretary
to a multi-millionaire, Heather's
stubborn loyalty to her former
flatmate plunges her into a grim
hazard.